"*I'm sorry I never really believed,*" I said. "*Not the way Jack did.*"

"It doesn't make any difference," my mother replied. Her eyes focused on the beanstalk for a moment, then returned to mine. "You believe now. Be safe and smart up there, my Gen. Be yourself."

Before I could answer, my mother turned away and walked quickly toward the house. I turned to face the beanstalk.

There is no going back now, I thought.

For better or worse, there was only going forward. There was only going *up*. Seizing the trunk of the beanstalk with both hands, I pushed off from the World Below and began to climb.

ONCE UPON A TIME

THE World Above

CAMERON DOKEY

SIMON PULSE
New York   London   Toronto   Sydney

SIMON PULSE

An imprint of Simon & Schuster Children's Publishing Division
1230 Avenue of the Americas, New York, NY 10020
First Simon Pulse paperback edition June 2010
Copyright © 2010 by Cameron Dokey
All rights reserved, including the right of
reproduction in whole or in part in any form.
SIMON PULSE and colophon are registered trademarks
of Simon & Schuster, Inc.
For information about special discounts for bulk purchases,
please contact Simon & Schuster Special Sales at
1-866-506-1949 or business@simonandschuster.com.
The Simon & Schuster Speakers Bureau can bring authors to your live event.
For more information or to book an event contact the Simon & Schuster
Speakers Bureau at 1-866-248-3049 or visit our website at
www.simonspeakers.com.
The text of this book was set in Adobe Jenson.
Manufactured in the United States of America
2 4 6 8 10 9 7 5 3 1
Library of Congress Control Number 2009938357
ISBN 978-1-4424-0337-6
ISBN 978-1-4424-0338-3 (eBook)

For Keek

PROLOGUE

Confession: I never intended to go looking for adventure. One came looking for me anyhow. And not just any old adventure. A really, really big one. The kind of adventure that changes your life. It certainly changed mine. Though, for the record, it was all Jack's fault.

Most things are.

Don't get me wrong. Jack is my brother, my twin, in fact, and I love him with all my heart. But if ever there was a magnet for adventure, or rather, *mis*adventure, Jack would be it. All during our childhood, he was forever getting into what our mother called "scrapes," most likely because a lot of scrapes (and also scratches) were actually involved.

Jack is my fraternal twin, not my identical twin, by the way. I'm a girl, not a boy. And before you leap to any conclusions, my name is not Jackie. It's Gen, short for Gentian, a wildflower that grows on the hills near the farm that is our home. Mama says she named me this because the gentian blossom is the exact same color blue as my eyes. Also the color of Jack's. Our hair, as long as I'm taking a moment to provide some physical description, is blond.

But here a difference arises. Jack's hair is a color that can only be described as golden. You know, like the sun. Mine is more like clover honey, a little darker and more serious. Just like the rest of me, my hair calls a little bit less attention to itself than Jack's does.

And this external feature, so easy to dismiss, actually reveals quite a lot about us. It provides a glimpse of who we are inside. Jack is the dreamer. I'm the planner. Jack is happiest when he's the center of attention. Me, I much prefer to stay in the background.

Which actually leads me back to where I started. Adventure. My having to go on one.

I began by climbing up a beanstalk.

I'm sure you're familiar with the story. Or at least you think you are. "Jack and the Beanstalk." That's what our tale is usually called. But there's a problem with that title. Actually, there's more than one. Whose name do you see there? Just Jack's. It doesn't mention me at all.

Not only that, it gives the impression there was only one beanstalk involved, when in fact there were many.

I'm thinking it's time to set the record straight. To share the true story. Not because I want to be the center of attention, but because the longer version of the tale is actually a whole lot more interesting than the shorter one.

My family, which consisted of Jack, our mother, and me, lived on a small farm. In good times we grew enough to feed ourselves and have some left to sell on market days in the nearest town. But we had not had a good year for several years running. The truth is that we were poor. So poor that one day we made a bitter decision: We had no choice but to sell our cow.

The cow's name was Agapanthus, something else most versions of our story leave out. And this is a shame, as Agapanthus is a pretty great name, as names for cows go. It's also a blue flower, just in case you were wondering. Agapanthus produced the sweetest milk for miles around. This made selling the cow herself a pretty good plan, even if none of us cared for it much. Jack cared for it least of all.

"But I don't want to sell her," he said. He, Mama, and I were standing in the barn. It had once contained several cows and an old horse to help pull the plow. Now only Agapanthus was left.

"I don't see why we have to," Jack went on now.

"Because it's the only option we have left," I said as patiently as I could. We'd been going over the same ground for what felt like hours. "We have to be able to plant, Jack. It's either that, or leave the farm. The money Agapanthus will bring should be enough to buy some clover seeds to help keep the fields healthy this winter, with enough left over to buy the seeds we need in spring as well. Then, if the weather will just cooperate and the crops do well—"

"Now who's being a dreamer?" Jack cut me off. "Neither of those things happened this year, not to mention last year, or the year before."

"Which isn't the same as saying they won't next year," I said, trying not to let my voice rise. "And *if they do*, we'll have enough to feed ourselves and take to market to sell besides, just like we used to. We might even earn enough money to buy Agapanthus back."

"Not very likely," Jack scoffed. He moved to throw an arm around the cow's neck, as if to protect her. Agapanthus butted her head against his shoulder. "Only a fool would let her go."

"Or someone desperate," I answered steadily. "A person brave enough to face the fact that they're out of options."

Jack opened his mouth to speak, but before he could, our mother intervened. "My children," she said. "Enough."

Jack shut his mouth with a snap, but he still glared at me. As far as he was concerned, the decision to sell the cow was all my doing. Hence, my fault.

"I don't like it any better than you do, Jack, but I think Gen is right," our mother went on. "We have to sell the cow. We can't afford to lose the farm. There is nowhere else for us to go."

There was a moment's silence while my mother's words hung in the air like dust. We all knew she was right. But knowing a difficult truth inside your head and hearing it spoken are two very different things.

"Then let me be the one to take her," Jack said, speaking up first and thereby foiling the plan I was about to propose: I should be the one to take the cow to market. Of the three of us, I would be able to obtain the most money for her. I drove the hardest bargains.

But now that Jack had spoken, I knew what our mother would decide. Though our outlook and temperaments were very different, Jack and I didn't actually argue all that often. Something about us being twins, I suppose. When we did disagree, however, our mother almost always took Jack's side.

"Very well," she said, agreeing to his proposal. "But be ready to take the cow to market first thing tomorrow morning."

And so, early the next day, still scowling to show how much he disapproved, Jack set off with Agapanthus. I probably don't have to tell you what happened next. Jack and the cow never made it to market. They didn't even make it all the way to town. Because along the way, Jack encountered an old woman who made him an offer he couldn't refuse: seven beans with mysterious and magical properties in exchange for our cow.

It's usually at this point that the storyteller pauses, allowing two things to happen: The storyteller gets to catch his or her breath, and the listeners have an opportunity to share their opinions about Jack's decision.

The general consensus is that my brother was an

idiot. Quite literally, a bean-brain. And it is most certainly true that when Jack came home that afternoon and revealed what he had done, our mother wept. This cannot be denied.

Tears of rage. Tears of despair. That's what most versions of our story tell you. But I'm here to tell you the truth. My mother's tears were neither of those things. Instead they were tears of joy.

My mother recognized those beans. She had waited a long time for them. Sixteen years to be precise, as long as Jack and I had been alive. She knew those beans were magic. Why? Because my mother had once planted a bean just like them herself, to grow a beanstalk of her own, a beanstalk that had saved all our lives.

You know those bedtime stories your parents told you when you were little? The ones populated by fairies and dragons, by damsels in distress and knights in shining armor? I hope you're sitting down. Because I'm here to tell you that they're all true. They just didn't happen in this world, the one where you and I were born and raised, the one my mother always called "the World Below." They happened in the land of my mother's birth, which should have been the land of Jack's and mine. A land of countless possibilities, including the ones that only magic can provide. A land that hovers out of sight, floating just above the clouds.

A land called the World Above.

My mother told bedtime stories too, of all shapes,

sizes, and varieties. But the one she told most often was the tale of how and why the first magic bean was planted, how its beanstalk came to grow, and why it was cut down. The tale of how we'd stopped being sky dwellers and had become residents of the World Below.

It begins the way all good tales do. With *Once upon a time . . .*

ONE

Once upon a time, a royal duke ruled over a small but prosperous kingdom. His name was Roland des Jardins. He was a wise and generous ruler, and his people flourished under his stewardship. There was only one cloud on the kingdom's horizon. Duke Roland was childless.

His duchess had died in childbirth many years before. The infant had perished also. Heartbroken by these events, Duke Roland had never remarried. By the time this story came to pass, the duke was getting on in years, though he was still hale and hearty. Still, it was a problem that he had no son to carry on the family name, no daughter to be the apple of her father's eye. You've probably heard enough stories like this to understand the reason why.

Without a child, girl or boy, the duke had no heir. No one to succeed him and rule when he was gone.

1

And when there's no clear contender for a throne, the less than clear ones always, well, *contend*. They compete and argue with one another. It's part of what the word means, after all. And all this uncertainty, this *contention*, meant that, although the duke's kingdom was at peace with its neighbors, it bore within it the spark to be at war with itself.

Now, there resided in Roland des Jardins' household a young nobleman named Guy de Trabant. Guy's father, Horace de Trabant, had been Duke Roland's closest childhood friend. He was also a duke, a ruler in his own right. His lands and those of Duke Roland bordered each other. It had been the two dukes' fondest hope that one day they would have children who would grow up to marry, thereby uniting the two kingdoms. Sadly, this dream had not come true.

First Roland des Jardins' wife died, and their infant child shortly thereafter. Then Horace de Trabant perished of the sweating sickness when his own son, Guy, was little more than a boy. As was the custom at that time, Duke Horace's widow sent her son to live with his father's friend, so that he might be raised in a duke's household and learn how to govern.

Many years went by. Guy de Trabant flourished under Duke Roland's care. He was everything a young nobleman should be. He was strong and handsome, brave in the face of his adversaries, generous to those less fortunate. He was, in fact, the old duke's successor in all but name. No one doubted that Duke Roland would name Guy de Trabant his heir. The two kingdoms would thereby be united, though admittedly not quite in the way that the two fathers had originally hoped.

Then something completely unexpected occurred. Roland des Jardins fell in love.

It happened at Guy de Trabant's wedding. Among the guests was a young woman named Celine Marchand. She was of good but minor birth, her father being a somewhat impoverished nobleman whose estate lay near the border of the de Trabant lands. Under ordinary circumstances, she might never have come to Duke Roland's attention at all. But the lady Celine was special. She had what they call "a way" about her. It didn't hurt, of course, that she was absolutely lovely.

Her hair was as blond as corn silk, her eyes as blue as a summer sky. She had one dimple in her chin and one in each of her cheeks when she smiled, which she did often. Her lips were full and red as ripe strawberries. Nor was this all. Lady Celine was also well-spoken, intelligent, and kind. Duke Roland fell in love at first sight, and the wonder of it was that Celine loved the duke as well.

So bright and shining was the love between them that not even the most cynical courtiers whispered that Celine Marchand had used artful wiles to snare a powerful older man in order to better her position in the world. All it took was one look at the couple to see that they were meant for each other.

Duke Roland and Lady Celine were married three months after Guy de Trabant. Then Roland des Jardins' subjects held their collective breath, praying for nature to take its course. For it seemed impossible that, after waiting so long for a second chance at happiness, the fates would not grant Duke Roland a child.

There was one person, of course, who, in his heart, could not bring himself to wish the old duke joy. Naturally, that person was Guy de Trabant. For if the new duchess bore a child, Guy's chance to become Duke Roland's heir would be over and done with forever.

If I'm to remain true to the way my mother always told the tale, this is where I must pause. I must gaze into space, as she always did, as though I can actually see events unfolding before my eyes. When I do this, I am using my imagination. But when my mother did it, she was looking back onto the scenes from her own life.

When she spoke of Celine Marchand, my mother was talking about herself.

It was always Jack who broke the silence, who brought my mother back to the here and now.

"What happened then, Mama?" he would ask, even though, by the time Jack was old enough to do this, we both knew the story by heart.

"What happened next?" my mother always echoed, as she pulled her attention back to the World Below. Sometimes her eyes held the sheen of tears, though never once did Jack and I see them fall.

"Injustice," my mother said. "That is what happened next, my son. Ingratitude begetting sorrow. I feel the wrongness of what happened as clearly today as I did long ago."

Desperate to obtain that which he had spent a lifetime believing would one day be his, Guy de Trabant had rallied the most contentious of Duke Roland's nobles in an attempt to seize the duke's crown. The battle for possession of the palace was brief but bloody. When it was over, the old duke lay dead, and the young man he had loved like a son was on his throne. But Guy de Trabant's rule could not yet be considered secure, for though the castle was searched from top to bottom not once, not twice, but three times, the duchess was nowhere to be found.

As it happened, she was less than a day's journey away. Duchess Celine had left early in the morning to visit her childhood nurse, an old wise woman named Rowan. The duchess had told no one but her husband of her plans. She had made the journey in the hope of confirming a suspicion that had recently taken root in her mind.

Duchess Celine believed she was with child.

By the time the duchess reached the wise woman's cottage, long shadows had begun to fall. Rowan helped the duchess tend to her horse, and then the two women went inside the cottage. They shared the evening meal together, and afterward the duchess insisted on doing all the washing up. Then, at long last, the two sat down before a bright and cheery fire, for although the day had been fine, the nights were beginning to turn cold.

"So," Rowan said after a few moments of contented silence. "How long have you known?"

At this the duchess gave a quick laugh. "I didn't *know*," she confessed. "Not for sure. Not until just now. It's why I came to see you. But I've suspected for almost a month."

"Your news will bring great happiness," Rowan said.

To which the duchess answered, "I hope so."

"Did I mention that it's twins?" the old wise woman asked. At which the duchess laughed once more.

"You know perfectly well you didn't," she replied. She rested a hand on her belly, as if she could already distinguish between the two children growing there. "Two," she said, her face thoughtful. "I hope it's one of each, a girl and a boy."

"Have you told Duke Roland yet?" the wise woman asked.

Celine shook her head. "No. I wanted to wait until I had seen you. I didn't want to raise false hopes."

It was at precisely that moment that a gust of wind blew down the chimney, sending out a shower of sparks. Startled, the two women leaped to their feet to stamp them out. But even when the sparks were extinguished, the wind was not. It prowled through the branches of the trees outside the house, making a noise that was a lament and warning all at once. The old wise woman cocked her head, as if the wind were speaking a language she could understand.

"What is it?" Celine asked, for the voice of the

wind was making her anxious. "What is wrong?"

"We must wait for the morning to know for sure, I think," her old nurse said. But she moved to take Celine's face between her hands and gazed into her eyes for a very long time. So long that the young woman began to tremble. For it seemed to her that, though her old nurse's hands were warm, and though the fire still burned in the grate, the room had suddenly grown cold. A cold that was finding a way inside her, burrowing straight toward her heart.

"No," she whispered. "No."

"Let us wait and see," the wise woman counseled. "By its very nature, wind is impetuous. Sometimes it exaggerates things or misunderstands."

But by the morning, the voice of the wind was not alone. Word of what had happened in the palace began to spread through the countryside, told by the hushed and fearful voices of Duke Roland's former subjects. In this way, the duchess learned that her worst fears had been realized. Her husband was dead. She herself was in great danger. Her unborn children were Duke Roland's true heirs. They must be protected at all costs.

"Ah, Roland! I should have told you," Celine whispered, as the tears streamed down her cheeks. "I wish I had. At least then you could have died with this joy in your heart."

"His heart was full of joy already," Rowan said. "For he loved you well."

"As I loved him," Celine replied.

At this the old woman gave a brisk nod. "Even so. Dry your eyes. You must not pour this love away in grief. You will need it to sustain you in what is to come. There is only one place where you and your children will be safe. You know that, don't you?"

Celine took the deepest breath of her life. She could feel it expanding her lungs, then streaming throughout her body, all the way down to the tips of her fingers and toes. She let it out and did a very unduchess-like thing. She wiped the sleeve of her dress across her face to dry her eyes. She squared her shoulders and lifted her chin.

"I know what must be done," Duchess Celine said. "Show me how to reach the World Below."

Two

In the end, it was simple. As simple as growing a beanstalk.

Both women knew there was no time to waste. Guy de Trabant would soon discover where the duchess had gone. Quickly but without letting their actions escalate their fear, Celine and Rowan made their preparations. First Rowan went into her kitchen and took a small green bowl down from the highest shelf. The two women peered inside. Nestled in the very bottom was a single bean, speckled red and white.

"Take this," Rowan instructed, as she upended the bowl, tipping the seed into Celine's palm. "Walk to the far end of my vegetable garden. Turn so that your back is to the meadow, and then throw the bean over your left shoulder. Don't look to see where it lands, but return to me at once."

Though her knees were inclined to wobble just a

little when she walked, Celine followed her old nurse's instructions. Her curiosity was great, but she did not turn around to see where the bean fell. Instead, as soon as the speckled seed had left her hand, she returned to the cottage.

"Work with me now," Rowan said. Together, the two women filled a large shawl with things to help Celine start a new life in the World Below.

Seeds from the wise woman's garden and orchard. A small pouch of gold coins. Various other sensible things it would be too long and boring to recount. Finally, though it made the bundle heavy, the wise woman added a hatchet. Then she tied the shawl twice. Once so that nothing could fall out, and a second time to make it nestle against the small of Celine's back, leaving her arms free for climbing. Finally she threw Celine's cloak over her shoulders and tied the drawstrings at the throat.

"Now," Rowan said, "let us go to the edge of the garden and see what has grown."

Together, the old woman and the young one walked to the place where the garden ended and a great meadow rolled beyond. The meadow was as flat as a pancake. At this time of year, summer just easing into fall, the grass was brown. But poking up through it was a sudden burst of bright green leaves covered with red speckles.

It was a beanstalk.

"Very good," the wise woman said. "That is fast work. It must have fallen onto fertile ground in the

World Below." For that is what the magic bean had done. It had slipped through the World Above and fallen all the way down to the World Below.

"We should give it a few more moments, I think. Just long enough to say good-bye."

The duchess threw her arms around her nurse and held on tight. Though the desire to weep filled her chest until she thought her heart would drown, she did not utter a single sound. She did not let a single tear fall.

"Listen to me, Celine," Rowan said. She swayed gently from side to side, rocking the grown woman as she once had the child. "I won't tell you not to feel bereft, not to be afraid. You will be both. But know this: You will not be forgotten. Always I will hold you in my heart.

"When the time is right, a messenger will come to the World Below. You and your children will be given the means to return to the World Above. It may be many years before this day comes, but never doubt that it will. Prepare your children well."

"I won't and I will," Celine said quietly. "I promise on the love I gave my husband."

"Then the time has come for you to climb down the beanstalk," Rowan said. The two women released each other. "When you reach the World Below, take out the hatchet and chop the beanstalk to the ground. Once you have done this, there will be no mark in this world to show where you have gone."

"But what if Guy de Trabant suspects?" Celine asked in a whisper.

Rowan gave a snort. "So what if he does? Guy de Trabant is going to have his hands full in this world. He will have no time to be worried about anything he might suspect of the World Below. You and your children will be safe there, Celine. Now trust me, and go."

And so the duchess Celine climbed down the beanstalk, down through the clouds and the wide-open sky, and alighted at last in the World Below. The moment her feet touched the ground, she immediately did as her old nurse had instructed. She took the bundle off her back, unfolded it, removed the hatchet, and chopped down the beanstalk.

It did not fall straight, as a tree might, but wound around in a great green coil, settling to the earth with a rustle and a sigh. The duchess gazed at the beanstalk in astonishment. For now that it lay on the ground, she could not imagine how it could have carried her from one world to another. It looked too thin, too delicate, too short. Yet all the while Celine had been climbing down, she had never doubted for a moment that the beanstalk would take her where she needed to go.

On impulse, she lifted it up and slipped it onto her shoulder. It seemed the proper thing to do somehow. Then she reknotted the shawl, slung it over the other shoulder, and looked around her. The beanstalk had taken her to a fold of gently rolling hills. In the distance, Celine thought she could see a ribbon of road.

"No time like the present," she murmured. With

determined steps, she began to make her way toward the road.

"And that is how we came to dwell in the World Below."

With this sentence, my mother always ended her story, blew out the candle, and kissed us good night. But Jack and I both knew what had followed. Our mother had used Rowan's gold coins to buy a farm not far from where she had first arrived in the World Below. It was close enough to a village that she did not feel all alone, but far enough away to be safe from prying eyes.

There, almost precisely eight months to the day after the events of her story, Jack and I were born. I was actually the first to put in my appearance, just in case you're wondering. My mother always said it explained my strange affection for the World Below. And this brings me to the most important difference between my brother and me.

Jack believed my mother's tale with his whole heart. He believed in the World Above. But try as I might, I could never quite bring myself to do so. My heart was too tied to the World Below.

Now, don't misunderstand me. I'm not calling my mother a liar. It's just that I could never make myself take her story for the *literal truth*. After all, she told it as a bedtime story. A way to lull Jack and me to sleep each night, so that we would be inspired when we awoke the next morning.

Everyone needs to believe that they are special,

different from those around them. That's what my mother's story always seemed like to me. A charm, a way to get us through hard times. But even as I appreciated the story she told, I never believed that it was true. Not the way Jack did, in his innermost heart of hearts.

That is, not until the day that Jack set off with Agapanthus and returned with a handful of beans instead of a pocketful of coins. Seven little beans, white with red speckles, the sight of which made my mother sit down abruptly in what was left of the carrot patch, laughing and crying at the same time.

That was when I realized my mother had meant every word of her bedtime story. It had been true, all of it. And I knew, in that moment, that nothing in our lives was ever going to be the same.

There would be a beanstalk in our future.

I could only hope I wouldn't have to be the one to climb it.

THREE

I needn't have worried. Jack was always going to be the one to go. It was actually something of a wonder he'd brought the beans home at all and hadn't simply tossed them over his shoulder immediately after he and the old woman completed their transaction.

For once in his life, however, Jack used his head. He kept it out of the clouds and squarely on his shoulders. Those beans were *important*. When a thing is important, you have to take extra care to get it right. That meant bringing the beans straight home to our mother.

"Well, my dears," my mother said. She dried her eyes but made no move to get up out of the carrot patch. "This is a momentous day, no two ways about it."

"That means it's a big deal," I said.

Jack made a rude sound. "I know what it means, Gen, thank you very much. I'm not the simpleton you'd like to make me out to be. I was smart enough to take the old woman's bargain, wasn't I?"

"Children, children," my mother said. But I could tell from the curve of her lips that she was holding back a smile. She extended a hand. As Jack's were full of beans, I was the one who reached out and helped her up.

"What do I have to do to grow a beanstalk?" Jack demanded, as soon as Mama was on her feet. "Just throw it over my left shoulder, right?" He turned and raised one arm as if to complete the action.

"Jack," my mother said, her voice like the snap of a whip. *"Stop right now."*

Jack's arm jerked to a stop, and his eyes went wide with astonishment. I might have been tempted to laugh if I hadn't been so surprised myself. Our mother never raised her voice.

"I'm sorry," Mama went on, in a tone I recognized. She moved to Jack and put a hand on his still upraised arm. Slowly he lowered it. "I didn't mean to sound so harsh, my son. But there are still many things you need to know before you can attempt a journey to the World Above."

Mama turned then and walked briskly toward the house.

"Come inside, both of you," she called over her shoulder. "We have many things to discuss."

"You might as well say it," I said as Jack and I fell into step together. "Otherwise you'll explode. Then I'll be the one who has to climb up some stupid beanstalk."

"It won't be stupid," Jack said. "It will be *stupen-*

dous." Before I realized what he intended, he caught me by both hands. "Think about it, Gen!" he cried, as he began to spin us both around. "Magic beans. Magic beanstalks."

"Jack," I protested, even as I caught his excitement. "You'll make me dizzy. Stop."

"Not until you confess you're a tiny bit interested in the World Above," he said. He leaned back, his hold on my hands the only thing keeping me from flying. "Come on, Gen. Come on."

"Oh, all right," I cried out. "Just a tiny little bit."

Jack stopped, pulling me to him in a breathless hug. I felt the way his heart beat, fast, against mine.

"Oh, and by the way," he whispered in my ear. "I told you so."

By the time we reached the house, Mama was seated in her favorite chair, by the window. In her lap she cradled the sugar bowl. It was one of the truly fine pieces that we owned, pristine white porcelain with a smattering of pale pink roses painted around its fat middle. The lid had a knob like a rosebud. Two handles stuck out like bent elbows on either side. Lovely as it was, we hadn't used the sugar bowl much lately. It had been empty for quite some time. Sugar is expensive, and we'd had no money to pay for such luxuries.

While I took a moment to wonder why on earth Mama was holding the sugar bowl, Jack seemed to grasp the significance at once. He tumbled the beans into it. They landed with a high, clattering sound. Mama put on the lid, then placed the bowl on the windowsill beside her chair. Now I could see that her lap contained another object as well, though I couldn't yet make out what it was.

"Sit down, children," my mother said. Jack and I settled down on the braided rug before her, our knees bumping together the same way they had when we were small.

"Tell me what you make of this, Gen," my mother went on. She held out the object she'd been holding in her lap. It was a piece of cloth. Somewhat surprised she hadn't offered it to Jack first, I took the scrap and held it up to the light.

"Well, it's wool, for starters," I said. I could tell that right off. Of the finest weave that I had ever seen or felt. The color appeared faded, but I thought it had once been a rich forest green.

"It is, indeed," my mother said. "It was once part of a cloak."

"Your cloak?" I asked quickly. "The one from the story? You mean this came from the World Above?"

Beside me, Jack shifted, as if holding back the impulse to snatch it away so he could examine it for himself.

My mother nodded. "As it turned out, I was glad Rowan insisted I bring it along. I cut it into baby blankets when you and Jack were born. But this piece I kept whole. Can you figure out why?"

"Because there's something on it," I said at once.

"It's embroidered." I squinted a little and leaned closer to the window. "It's a shield, quartered." The scrap of cloth fell from my hands and into my lap as the realization hit. "It's a coat of arms."

At this, Jack decided he'd had enough. "Let me see it," he demanded. I handed him the scrap of wool, the images I'd seen whirling through my mind.

The upper left-hand corner of the shield showed a sack overflowing with gold coins. Beside the sack, upper right, was a bird with its wings spread open wide. In the lower left, below the sack, was a type of harp called a lyre.

I knew it was a lyre because I can actually play one. To tell you the truth, I play pretty well. I was taught by a traveling musician who came to our village for one of the harvest festival celebrations. I'd been so intrigued, I'd attended every single performance. Delighted by the young girl who'd watched his performance so intently, the musician had asked Mama's permission to give me lessons. He'd even gone so far as to give me the gift of an old instrument when he moved on to another town.

Mama always claimed that my love of music was proof that I was my father's daughter, proof of my ties to the World Above. I finally thought I understood.

In the lower right corner of the shield was a beanstalk.

All of a sudden, I sat up a little bit straighter. "Jack," I said. "Let me see that again."

"Why?" Jack countered at once, as much out of

habit as anything else. "Did you see the beanstalk?"

"That's why I want it back," I said.

Scowling, a surefire sign he was curious but would never admit it, Jack handed over the scrap of wool. Again I held it up to the light.

"The beanstalk is newer than the other images," I said. I lowered the cloth and looked into my mother's face. *The face of the woman in her stories,* I thought. *The face of a woman once named Celine Marchand.* There was the single dimple in her chin, but until today it had been a long time since I had seen my mother smile. The World Below had offered its protection, but life here had not always been kind.

"*You* added the beanstalk," I said. "After coming to the World Below."

The dimples in my mother's cheeks put in a brief appearance. *She is so beautiful, still so beautiful when she smiles,* I thought. No wonder the father I had never known had fallen in love with her at first sight.

"I wondered how long it would take you to notice that," my mother said. "You're right. I stitched the beanstalk that first winter, while I was waiting for you and Jack to be born."

"Before or after you cut the cloak up for our blankets?"

The dimples put in another swift appearance. "Before. It was a cold winter. The cloak covered my lap and helped to keep me warm."

"But what does it all mean?" Jack demanded. "Why wait to tell us now?"

"These are the symbols of our family's power," my mother replied. "Of the covenant between us and those we once governed. I didn't tell you about them before because . . ." She paused.

"Because they were so specific," I said suddenly. I was good at solving puzzles. It was part of my ability to make a plan.

I glanced sidelong at Jack. "Specific enough to give us away if someone I know couldn't keep quiet about them."

"Hey," Jack protested.

"I'm sorry to say this, Jack," our mother told him. "But Gen is right. You do have a tendency to speak before you think, no matter who's around."

I wasn't sure who was more surprised, Jack or I. Mama almost never criticizes him, perhaps because they're so close. Even when she does point out some flaw, she almost always lets Jack off the hook with little more than a scolding.

"It's just part of my exuberant nature," Jack said with a grin. When he does that, he has the same two dimples in his cheeks as Mama.

Mama sighed. *Here we go again,* I thought. Those dimples, so much like her own, get her every time. I just have the one in my chin. It's less charming, apparently, since you can see it all the time.

"So it is," she said. "And that is one of the things I love best about you, as you well know." Jack had the grace to look down. "But pay attention. Gen really does have a point.

"A country lad boasting of being more than what he seems is nothing special. There are lads all over the World Below who do. Lads whose dreams are larger than the circumstances of their lives. But a lad who boasts and can back it up by describing his family's coat of arms, that kind of a lad calls a particular kind of attention to himself, attention we still cannot afford."

Jack frowned. He rubbed his fingers over the ridges in the braided rug.

"All right," he finally acknowledged. "I see the point."

The point, I noticed. Not *Gen's* point. I bit down on my tongue.

"Why are these symbols on our coat of arms, Mama?" I said instead. "How did our family come by them?"

"That is a good story too," our mother said. "One I've long wished to tell you.

"Many years ago, one of your father's ancestors gave shelter to a wizard. He did this out of the goodness of his heart, without knowing who the man was. In gratitude, the wizard gave him three magical gifts designed to help him govern wisely and well.

"The first was a sack of gold with the power to refill itself, a demonstration of the way a kingdom will prosper when it is justly governed. The second was a goose who could lay eggs with yolks so rich and golden that, even if all the crops in the kingdom should fail, the people would never go hungry. The third was a harp with a voice so pure it could speak the truth of its own accord. Your father's ancestor accepted the gifts with thanks. Then he incorporated them into the family's coat of arms."

"But what about the beanstalk?" Jack asked.

"I am coming to that," said my mother. "It turned out that the wizard had a fourth gift to bestow, one not as pleasant as the others. He looked into the future and saw that a great sadness would befall our house. He could not see precisely how it would come about, or even what it was. So the wizard made a prophecy, which was also something of a riddle:

"'That which has taken you away from all you love will also be the means to restore you.' Your father's ancestor then decreed that the final quarter of the shield must be left blank until the riddle could be solved."

"A beanstalk," I murmured, brushing my fingers over the stitches my mother had made.

"A beanstalk," my mother agreed, nodding.

"But it was Guy de Trabant who took everything you loved away," Jack protested. "Not that I'd want to see his face on our family coat of arms."

"That's not what the prophecy said," I countered before Mama could respond. "It doesn't say, 'that which has taken what you love away from you,' it says 'that which has taken you away from all you love.'"

"Even so," my mother said. "And the thing that did that was a beanstalk. Now, at last, the second part of the wizard's prophecy has come true. Jack's beans will provide us with the means to return to the World Above."

My mother rose to her feet, her blue eyes shining with a light that I had never seen there before.

"But we will not stop there, my children. We will not simply return. We will do more. We will drive the usurper Guy de Trabant from our lands. We will reclaim what is rightfully ours!"

FOUR

There was a silence so profound you could have heard a feather drop.

"*How?*"

My mother's brow furrowed. "What?"

"There, you see? That's just it!" I cried, surging to my feet. "*How* are we supposed to reclaim all that is rightfully ours? Guy de Trabant has already killed to claim a kingdom. He's hardly going to welcome us with open arms."

"Well, we'll just have to think of something," Jack said. He stood up too and stepped to Mama's side, wrapping a possessive arm around her shoulders. "We'll think of a way."

"Yes," I said. "But how will we know if what we think up is possible? It's been sixteen years since Mama escaped. All we know are the old stories. None of us has any idea what's happened in the World Above during her absence. It is possible Guy de Trabant could actually be dead."

"No," my mother said at once, absolute certainty in her tone. She gave Jack's shoulder a pat. He released her and stepped away. "I know it doesn't make much sense, but if he had ceased to breathe, I believe that I would know."

"All right, we'll take it as a given that he's still alive," I said. "Alive and in control. He must have friends."

Jack made a rude sound.

"Okay, perhaps not friends," I said. "But surely he has allies. People he feels he can count on if trouble arrives. We have no one. We don't *know* anyone. We don't know what's going on."

"Then that's our plan right there," Jack said, his tone triumphant. "One of us must go to the World Above, first to gather information about the current state of affairs, second to see if anyone might be persuaded to join our cause. It can be—what do you call it—a reconnaissance mission."

"You mean *you'd* be going," I said.

"So what if I do?" Jack countered. "I found the beans, didn't I? I was the one who saw the chance and took it. You'd never have done that in a million years. You wouldn't have given that old woman the time of day. Oh, you'd have been polite. No doubt about that. But you wouldn't have listened. You wouldn't have *wanted* to listen. You'd have kept right on going, and our chance to return to the World Above would have been lost."

"Why must you always try to put me in the wrong?" I asked. "Just because I don't see what's so bad about the World Below?"

"I'm not trying to put you in the wrong," Jack said. "I'm trying to make a point."

"What?"

Jack dragged frustrated fingers through his hair. "You just said it yourself: You don't see what's so bad about the World Below. For the record, I never said anything was. But here's the difference between us, Gen. *You don't see what might be special about the World Above.* You don't want to. You never even really believed it was real until now.

"That's why I should be the one to go. Because I want to. Because I've always wanted to. Because I believe in the World Above."

"Okay," I said, trying to ignore the way his words stung. "Let's say you're right. I have a point too, Jack, and it's just as good as any of yours. All you can do is gather information and come right back home. Nothing more. No getting distracted. *No adventures.* There's too much at stake."

Jack's face flushed. "I know what's at stake," he said. "Stop treating me like a child."

"Enough!" my mother finally cried, silencing us. "Both of you make good points. I agree with Jack. He is the right one to go. But I also agree with Gen. You must proceed with caution, my son."

She stepped forward and laid a hand on each of our shoulders. "This opportunity will be a challenge for both of you," she said. "Though for different reasons. For you, Jack, perhaps because you want it too much. And for you, Gen, because you want it too little. Your heart is so tied to the World Below."

"What's so wrong about that?" I asked, my voice small, even to my own ears.

"Only this," my mother replied. "It may be your place of birth, but it is not your true home, my Gen. That place must be the World Above. The World Above is the keeper of your past. Until you have seen it for yourself, you cannot know where your future lies."

"And in the present," Jack broke in, "there is still the small matter of growing a magic beanstalk."

My mother laughed suddenly, the sound as bright and clear as the light on a summer morning. She caught us close to her in a hug.

"My children, my children, what am I going to do with you?" she inquired with a smile. "One wants to drag her feet, while the other can't wait to fly."

She released us, and we all took a step back.

"Well, Gen? What do you think? What plan shall we make to satisfy Jack's desire to grow a magic beanstalk?"

"I think you mean *giant* magic beanstalk," I said. "Which means we should call as little attention to it as possible."

"You can't be serious," Jack protested.

"I'm absolutely serious," I said. "You have to wait for nightfall."

ᗡ ᗡ ᗡ

Jack tossed the first bean over his shoulder just as the moon began to rise. After additional discussion, it had been decided that the cornfield was the perfect place to grow a magic beanstalk.

The field was tucked between two of the many hills surrounding our farm. This would make the beanstalk difficult to see from a distance, and if someone did notice that one stalk in the cornfield seemed a bit taller than the rest, well, what of it? With the breeze moving through the field, causing the cornstalks to sway and dance, anything different could be dismissed as nothing more than a trick of the light.

It is difficult to get people in the World Below to see what they don't expect to see. Mama has remarked on this more than once. Even I have to admit it's true. Now we would make this fact work for our cause.

And so, just as the pale face of the moon peered up over the horizon, Jack and I walked to the cornfield while Mama stayed in the house. I think both Jack and I were surprised that Mama didn't come along. But she'd instructed us to go together. So that's what we did, traversing the distance between the house and the cornfield in absolute silence. At the edge of the field, Jack paused, then turned his back to the rows of corn.

"Count for me, will you?" he asked. He gave a sudden, sheepish grin. "I know it's only to three, but I'm terrified I'm going to get it wrong, somehow."

For once I didn't tease him. Probably because I knew exactly how he felt.

"On three, then," I said.

Jack nodded.

"One. Two. *Three.*"

With one quick, smooth motion, Jack tossed the bean over his left shoulder.

I swore I saw it flying through the air, a tiny white speck tumbling end over end against the darkened sky. But in the interests of truth, I must admit that I might have made this up. It could have been a trick of the light combined with my own desire. As Jack let the bean fly, the wind came up, causing the cornstalks to rustle and sway, almost as if they were conversing with one another.

Jack stood for a moment, his hands clenching and unclenching at his sides. I saw his chest heave and realized he was breathing hard, as if he'd run a race and put on a final burst of speed to reach the finish line.

"Don't do it, Jack," I said suddenly. "Don't turn around."

For Mama had said that it was important to let magic run its own course. Trying to influence it could spell disaster. For this reason, Jack must not look back. He must not watch to see where the bean had fallen. I could do so, Mama said, as I was not the one who would be climbing the beanstalk.

"I know," Jack said. "I know."

I moved to his side and took him by the arm. He was quivering, his whole body vibrating like one of the plucked strings on my harp.

"Let's go in," I said softly. "We'll come back at first light."

Jack reached out to grasp me by both elbows. "It's happening, Gen. It's really happening. I'm going to go to the World Above."

"You're going to go to the World Above," I said. "Always assuming some crow didn't get to that bean as soon as it hit the ground."

Jack gave a sudden laugh. I felt the tension leave his body.

"Good old Gen," he said. "Always trying to make sure I don't get too far ahead of myself."

"Self-defense," I said. "Slowing you down's the only way I can keep up."

"Don't be ridiculous," Jack said. He pulled me forward into a fierce hug. "I love you."

"I love you, too," I said as I hugged him back. We stepped apart and I put my hands on Jack's shoulders, the better to peer up into his face.

"Jack, you will be careful, won't you?"

"Of course I'll be careful," he said. Then he made a face. "At least I'll try. But you heard Mama, Gen. Ultimately, we are going back to reclaim what Guy de Trabant stole from us. Sooner or later, there are bound to be some risks involved."

He broke free of my hold to take a few steps away. Jack literally thinks best on his feet, preferably when he's using them to go somewhere.

"I just wish I could figure out a way to prove who I am—who we are," he went on. "I don't want people to think I'm just another usurper."

I hesitated a moment. "I've been thinking about that too," I acknowledged.

Jack spun back around. Before I realized what he intended, he caught me up in his arms, twirling me around.

"You've got a plan, don't you?" he cried. "I knew it. I knew I could count on you. I knew you wouldn't let me down."

"No, I don't have a plan." I gasped, clinging to his shoulders as air filled my skirts like a bell. "Not a full-fledged one, anyhow. It's just an idea, Jack. Now put me down."

"*Full-fledged?*" Jack echoed with a laugh. But at least he set me down. "Who in the World Below says stuff like that?"

"Clearly," I said as I did my best to smooth my hair and skirts, "only someone who comes from the World Above. And it was never my intention to let you down. I don't know why you have to say a thing like that."

Jack sobered. "I'm sorry," he said. "I didn't mean that the way it sounded."

"You're Mama's favorite," I told him, the words tumbling out before I could stop them. "We both know it's true, so don't bother to deny it. It's because of the way I feel about the World Below. But I'm just as much a part of this family as you are, Jack. I'd never let you down."

I began to stomp my way back to the house.

"Gen, wait," Jack said. I heard the quick sound

of his feet. "I didn't mean it like that. You're making too much of it. How come we've spent the whole day fighting? I don't want us to."

"I don't want us to fight either," I said. I stopped walking as the extent of the truth of this struck me.

"Then what *do* you want?"

"I want you to come home safe," I said.

"I want that too," Jack said. "But what if home turns out to be the World Above?"

"It doesn't make a difference," I said. "I just want you to be safe, that's all. I don't want you to end up sacrificed to Guy de Trabant's ambition like our father was."

Or your own ambition, for that matter, I thought.

"I'll be careful. I swear I will," Jack vowed. "Just say you'll do one thing for me."

"What's that?"

"Wish me luck."

"Good luck, Jack," I said. And I meant it with all my heart.

That was the moment I felt it. I can't explain how. I felt the magic take root and the beanstalk begin to grow.

"You know," Jack said as he slung an arm around my shoulders, "we make a pretty good team, whether you like to admit it or not. You provide the plan; I provide the quick thinking if anything goes wrong."

I gave a snort. "Which it almost always does. Could that be because you change the plan the minute it's made? Wait a minute. Yes, I do believe that could account for it."

Jack gave my shoulders a quick, hard squeeze. "Cut it out."

"If you're trying to ask me whether or not I've been figuring out a way for you to prove who you really are, the answer is yes," I said. "It has to do with our family's coat of arms. . . ."

FIVE

Jack and I talked well into the night, whispering with our heads together and our bodies stretched out in opposite directions on the soft braided rug. We'd often done this when we were small, on winter nights when the warmest place to sleep was in front of the fire. Just as the sun came up, Jack shook me awake.

"Wake up, sleepyhead," he said. "Come see what's in the cornfield."

Five minutes later Jack, Mama, and I stood gazing up into the leaves of an enormous beanstalk.

I'd known it would be there. Hadn't I felt the moment it began to grow? Even so, it was hard to believe a vine could stretch up and up and up until it was lost to sight among the clouds. It swayed ever so slightly in the early morning breeze; its red and green speckled leaves made a strangely soothing sound. The stalk itself was as wide around as Jack was, as if it had been custom grown. Which, of course, it had.

"It's beautiful," breathed my mother.

"It is," I acknowledged. I bit down on my tongue. It didn't do any good. "It's also impossible!" I burst out. "Jack can't climb that. It will never hold him."

"One just like it held me," my mother reminded me.

"But Mama—"

"It's all right, Gen," Jack interrupted to silence me. "It may look impossible. But somehow I think that it's supposed to. The World Above and the World Below aren't supposed to be joined together. People aren't supposed to travel back and forth. To do so takes courage. It takes—"

"A leap of faith," I finished for him on a sigh. My mother made an approving sound. She moved to stand between us, linking arms, so that we formed a chain. Together, we all stood gazing at the beanstalk. It flicked its leaves at us, as if waving hello.

"You should go soon, Jack," Mama said softly. "The sun is almost up."

"I'm really going to do it," Jack said, his voice reverent. "I'm going to climb a magic beanstalk."

Twenty minutes later all was in readiness. Jack had wolfed down a breakfast of all his favorite foods, then settled the pack he and Mama had prepared onto his shoulders. The three of us returned to the cornfield and the beanstalk.

"What will we do if someone comes by?" I asked suddenly.

"Easy," Mama declared stoutly. "We'll simply pretend the beanstalk isn't there."

I gave a startled laugh. "Mama, that will never work. Not even our neighbors are that gullible."

"Don't be so sure," my mother answered. "If there's one thing people in the World Below hate, it's for others to think they're foolish. If we pretend the beanstalk isn't there, it won't be. You mark my words.

"People in the World Above, on the other hand," she continued, turning to Jack, "expect to be surprised. That's why your best course of action will be to be precisely what you seem, my son."

Jack made a face. "A country bumpkin."

"Better a live country bumpkin than a dead nobleman," my mother said bluntly. She laid a hand on Jack's shoulder. "Do just as we discussed. Find out as much as you can about the current situation, then come right back. After that, we can put Gen to work on a plan."

Jack raised a hand to cover Mama's, giving it a squeeze. "I know what to do, Mama. I'll be careful, I promise."

"Then I wish you luck, my son."

Jack turned and met my eyes. "I'll be back soon," he said.

"I'll be waiting for you," I replied.

Without another word, Jack strode to the beanstalk and laid a hand against its trunk. I saw the way he leaned against it, as if testing his weight against its strength. Then he tipped his head back, as if he could already see the World Above, floating somewhere high above him. His face filled with emotion. Never in all my life, neither before nor since, have I seen more joy than I did in Jack's face the instant before he began to climb that beanstalk.

Good luck, Jack, I thought. *I love you.*

Jack set a foot against the trunk, wrapped his arms around it, and boosted himself up. Then, just as if he was climbing a tree, he began to climb the beanstalk. Mama and I stood watching as he made his way into the sky, until the light of the sun made tears fill our eyes and we had no choice but to look down.

SIX

Jack was gone all that day, and the next one as well. Mama and I did our best to keep ourselves busy. On the first day, we cleaned the house from top to bottom. Sheets washed, bedding aired, floors swept and scrubbed, windows polished until they sparkled. Mama even tied her biggest apron around her oldest dress and blacked the stove. By the time we tumbled into bed that night, I was so tired that I had no choice but to sleep soundly. Yet all through the night, I dreamed of beanstalks.

On the second day, I worked in the kitchen vegetable garden, just as I did every autumn. Turning over the soil in the beds, trying to inspire the dry soil with my care so that better times might come. My mother stayed in the kitchen, making the little we had go as far as possible, working the only kind of magic she had ever been able to conjure up in the World Below.

The shadows lengthened until at last it was too dark for me to stay outdoors any longer, until my mother had to light the lamps and cover the dishes of food she'd prepared, and still Jack had not come home. I washed my hands and we sat together in the kitchen, making a meal of cheese and bread and apples.

How much longer? I wondered. How long did it even take to reach the World Above?

How long before Mama and I decided that Jack was in trouble? How long before one of us had to go up after him to find out what was wrong?

After supper, I washed the dishes. By mutual yet silent consent, Mama and I remained in the kitchen. Mama brought out her sewing, while I prepared a goose quill pen and set to making a list of what I hoped to plant next spring—and the neighbors from whom I hoped to acquire the seed to do so. Then I added a third column: what I might be able to barter for the seed, as it seemed unlikely we'd be able to pay for it. The scratch of the sharpened quill against the paper was the only sound in the room.

"What are you doing, Gen?" my mother asked finally.

Her voice sounded rusty, as if she'd forgotten the use of it in just one day.

"I'm making a list," I answered, hoping to discourage further discussion. I was pretty sure my mother was hoping we wouldn't still be here in the spring. She was hoping we'd be back where she thought we belonged—in the World Above.

Mama sighed. "I can see that you're making a list," she said mildly. "I was hoping you'd care to share what kind."

I explained. My mother's hands paused, her needle poised above the sewing. Then she plunged the sharp point into the fabric.

"You're planning pretty far ahead, aren't you?"

Somebody around here has to, I thought. *Someone willing to admit we might all still be living here next spring.*

"I have to, Mama," I said instead. "It's my nature."

Mama set her sewing down on the table and reached across its smooth, scrubbed surface to lay a hand on my arm.

"I know it is, sweetheart. Your father was just the same." She sighed again, and I thought it sounded sad this time. "Perhaps I should have told you before now."

I felt a strange tightness wrap itself around my chest.

"You hardly ever talk about Papa at all," I said. "Except in your bedtime stories."

"I know," my mother said quickly. "And I'm sorry for it. I didn't mean *not* to speak of him, it's just—"

But what she would have said next I never knew, for at precisely that moment, the kitchen door flew open. Jack stood on the threshold. In one hand he clutched an all but empty sack. Cradled in the nook of his other arm was the sorriest excuse for a goose I'd ever seen in my life. My mother stood up so quickly, her chair tipped over backward.

"Jack!" she cried. "Thank goodness you're home! What have you done?"

"What Gen and I planned that I would do, if I had the chance," Jack said simply, though I could see the way his chest heaved as if he'd been running. He set the sack on the table with a faint *chink* and extended the goose toward my mother even as his eyes met mine.

"Gen," my brother said, "I wonder if you'd be so good as to go and chop down the beanstalk."

"Take the lantern," my mother said as she reached for the bedraggled goose. "It's dark. There, sweetheart," she went on, as she took the exhausted creature into her arms. "You know me, don't you? There now. It's going to be all right."

"There's some food on the sideboard," I said to Jack. Snatching up the axe, I went out into the night and closed the door behind me.

When I came back, Jack and Mama were seated across from each other at the table. The loaf of bread Mama had baked was half eaten. The cheese was gone. The goose was wrapped in a blanket and tucked into an old apple picking basket beside my mother's feet. It seemed to hold its head up a little more strongly, I thought.

"Gen," Jack said as I came in. I returned the axe to its place near the stove. Chopping down the beanstalk had been easier than I expected. Now that Jack was once more safe in the World Below, it was almost as if the beanstalk had *wanted* to be chopped down.

"Mama made pie! If you want a piece, you'd better come and cut it now. The only time I can remember being as hungry as this was after I climbed *up* the beanstalk."

"Is everything all right?" my mother asked. It was a general enough question, but I knew what she meant. There'd been nobody on the beanstalk when I chopped it down. No one trying to follow Jack back to the World Below.

"Fine," I replied. I approached the table, and Mama cut me a slice of pie.

"Hey, wait a minute," Jack said, as if he'd suddenly realized something. "I thought there wasn't any sugar. How can there be pie?"

"A mother has to have some secrets," Mama said with a smile.

"Jack," I said, pulling the plate with my slice of pie on it toward me. It was a large piece, I was happy to note. "Shut up and eat. Or if you have to talk, tell us about the World Above. I know the plan was to try and reclaim the wizard's gifts, but I never dreamed you would do it so quickly. How did you manage it?"

"I didn't, not really," Jack confessed. He took an enormous bite of pie, chewing slowly as he savored the taste. It was apple, his favorite and mine. "It was Shannon and Sean."

"Shannon and Sean?" my mother asked sharply. "Who are they?"

Jack dished up another forkful of pie. "Sean is a

giant, and Shannon is the most beautiful girl I've ever seen, Mama. They're brother and sister, though you'd never know it to look at them. Shannon's not much taller than Gen is, while Sean towers over me. They live in the castle that used to be Duke Roland's. It's kind of a long story."

I took a bite of pie. It was perfect, simple as it was. And all of a sudden I found myself afraid. What if there was nothing as wonderful yet simple as this in the World Above? Mama wanted us to return to the World Above to reclaim all our family had lost, not least of which was a kingdom and a crown.

But would returning to the World Above take things away as well? Things we wouldn't even know were valuable until after they were gone? Like the ability to sit together in the kitchen, enjoying a well-made piece of pie.

"Tell us your story, Jack," my mother said.

And so Jack began to tell of his journey up the beanstalk into the World Above.

SEVEN

"I climbed almost all day," Jack said. "Or at least I think I did. It was almost dark by the time I reached the World Above. And the funny thing was that I ended up in a cornfield, just like where I'd started out. I even had one moment where I thought I'd gone terribly wrong somehow and had ended up back in the World Below.

"Then I saw Sean. After that, I was pretty sure I was in the right place."

"But why would Guy de Trabant go to all the trouble to steal our father's castle only to abandon it to a family of giants?" I inquired.

"I asked Sean that very question," Jack answered, as he took another bite of pie. "He couldn't say, for certain. He was just a baby when his family first moved in. Sean and Shannon's father, Clarence, was the giant Guy de Trabant chose."

"Perhaps de Trabant couldn't live with himself," I surmised. "He couldn't bear to live in the castle he'd killed for. He didn't need to. He had one of his own. One he could inhabit without guilt. And it's not as if he gave up Duke Roland's lands. He still kept those."

"I think you're right on all counts, Gen," my mother put in quietly. "Not only that, the de Trabant castle is built like a fortress. I saw it once, as a child. It's situated at the crest of a hill, if I remember correctly. No one can approach without being seen. Guy de Trabant would have felt, and been, well protected there."

"And in the meantime," I filled in thoughtfully, "to make sure no other ambitious man would try to steal from him, he installed a giant in Duke Roland's castle."

"I think that must be it," Jack agreed.

"But where did he find a giant in the first place?" I wondered. "Where did Clarence come from?"

"I asked Sean and Shannon about that," Jack said. "And they said their father never spoke about his origins. It was one of two topics that they were forbidden to mention. The other was their mother, who died when they were born. They didn't come right out and say this, but I gathered things were kind of grim when Shannon and Sean were growing up. This only fed the stories about a ferocious giant living in the castle."

"Stories that Guy de Trabant had no doubt started himself, to discourage other potential usurpers," I said.

Jack nodded. "But something happened to Clarence as time went by," he went on. "Shannon said she thought her father fell in love. Not with another person, but with many. He fell in love with Duke Roland's former subjects. He saw the way they struggled to make ends meet, yet still kept their spirits strong. He discovered that he wanted to be more than just a tool to frighten others. He wanted to belong. He wanted his children to feel as if they had a true home.

"So, slowly but surely, Clarence set to work to rebuild the land that Guy de Trabant had first stolen and then abandoned to neglect. As they grew old enough, Sean and Shannon helped him. Father and son traveled from village to village, helping with the harvest, or mending a broken roof or fence, whatever needed to be done. Shannon stayed on in the castle, where she tended an enormous vegetable garden."

Jack smiled at me. "You'd like that about her, Gen. In fact, I think you'd just plain like *her*. Shannon reminded me of you, right off. She's no-nonsense, practical, and straightforward."

"Don't forget the most beautiful girl you've ever seen," I teased.

Jack colored.

"Is Clarence still alive?" my mother asked.

Jack shook his head. "No. He died about a year ago. All Duke Roland's former subjects mourned him. Since then, Sean and Shannon have stayed on in the castle, carrying on in their father's footsteps."

"It's a lovely story," I said. "Filled with hope. But why would total strangers tell you their life story, Jack? Why would they think you wanted to know it?"

Jack winced, as if he'd known this question was coming. "You're not going to like this," he said. "They told me their story because I told them mine."

I sat bolt upright in horror. "*What?* The whole idea was to keep your identity a secret!"

"I know," Jack replied in a pleading tone. "But if you'd been there, you'd have done the same, Gen. I just know it. There was just something about them . . . it's as if they already knew me somehow. And then, when I saw the goose and recognized her as one of the wizard's gifts, that sort of settled things. I told them my story, and they told me theirs. Afterward they brought out the sack of coins. Guy de Trabant had left it behind too."

"It seems strange that he would leave the wizard's gifts," I said more calmly. "I wonder why."

"Perhaps they reminded him of the wrongs he had committed, the ones he is still committing," my mother suggested in a hard voice. She gestured toward the goose in its basket at her feet. It was sleeping now, its head tucked beneath one wing. It looked peaceful, but exhausted. The sack of coins lay flat on the table beside the empty pie plate. To look at the sack, you would have thought that it was empty as well.

"All you have to do is look at either of these things to know that something is terribly wrong with the way our former kingdom is being governed. Or, more accurately, not governed," my mother went on. "My guess is that Guy de Trabant didn't want these reminders of his failure."

"What about the lyre?" I asked. "Did he leave that as well?"

Jack shook his head. "No. That's the one thing Guy de Trabant took with him. Rumor has it that he almost never lets it out of his sight, and that he uses the lyre to help govern his own people, rather than using his own judgment."

Jack ate the last forkful of pie, then pushed his plate away as if his hunger had finally been satisfied.

"Winning back the lyre is going to be a challenge."

"One you think you know how to meet," I said. The look on Jack's face told me he'd been doing something out of character. He'd been developing a plan of his own.

"Not yet, but I think I know how to discover if a *how* is even possible," Jack replied.

Mama leaned in, suddenly intent. "What are you thinking, Jack?" she asked.

"Twice a month, Guy de Trabant holds a court of assizes. Any of his subjects may come before him to present a grievance or a matter that needs to be settled."

"And de Trabant uses the harp to help him pass judgment," I said.

"That's it, precisely." Jack nodded. "If I could find a way—"

"Are you mad?" I broke in before he could complete the thought. "Think of all the people who might see you, not to mention the soldiers. Both de Trabant and the harp are bound to be heavily guarded. We don't even really know what the fortress looks like. We know it's on top of a hill, but what else? Even assuming you could manage to get to the harp, how would you escape with it?"

"Thank you for asking me the same questions I've been asking myself," Jack said testily. "How is this helping?"

"It helps to clarify just what you're up against, Jack," Mama said.

"I know what I'm up against," Jack said stubbornly. He looked between the two of us, his gaze finally settling on our mother. "Don't you even want me to try? I thought this was what you wanted me to do, Mama. To return to the World Above and reclaim all that is rightfully ours."

"And so I do," replied our mother. "But . . ." She paused, trying to select the right words. "These last couple of days, while Gen and I waited, I came to understand what it would mean to lose you. I want you to take your place as your father's rightful heir with all my heart, Jack. I want to see you sitting on his throne. But I want to keep you alive and well more. If you were to be captured or killed—"

"I won't be," Jack said in quick reassurance, reaching across the table to grasp her hand. "I won't be, Mama."

"Then listen to your sister," Mama said. "She wants you to succeed as much as I do."

"Of course I do," I said quietly. "Though you know . . . officially, I'm the rightful heir to the throne, not you. I am five minutes older. And there's nothing that says a girl can't succeed."

Jack's mouth dropped open, as did Mama's. I might have been tempted to laugh, were it not for the twist of pain in my heart. Sensible Gen, boring Gen with her strange affection for the World Below. Who would have considered her for a crown in the World Above?

"Fortunately for you," I went on, "I have no desire to sit on a throne. But if that's what *you* want, then we should get you there in one piece."

Jack took a deep breath, then let it out slowly, as if expelling his preconceived notions along with his breath.

"All right, then," he said. "What did you do with that pen and paper, Mama?"

"I put them on the sideboard."

Jack fetched the inkpot, quill, and paper I'd been using earlier, then returned to the table. He placed the paper on the table, turning the sheets over so that my handwriting was facedown. If he'd noticed the nature of the lists I'd been making, he gave no sign. He opened the inkpot and dipped the quill into the ink.

"Now," he said, "I am going to pretend I'm Gen. I'm going to make a list of all the things we think I need to find out before I attempt to win back the lyre. That will be one column. All the potential pitfalls will go in another. Then I'll return to the World Above and get our questions answered. I'll add more as they come up. I'll do whatever it takes to create a plan we believe can be successful.

"But you have to understand something." He looked at me and then our mother. "If I'm going to do this, if I'm really going to win back Roland des Jardins' crown, then sooner or later, I'm going to have to take a risk. There's simply no way around it. Either you trust me to take the right chance at the right time, or you don't. And if you don't, I'll do this completely on my own. My plan, my risk, my chance to win back what's rightfully ours."

"*Ours*," I replied. "That's the key word, Jack. Of course I want to help you. What you're doing is for all of us." I slid the paper in front of me, then extended my hand, palm up, for the quill.

"You should let me write the list," I said. "Your handwriting is atrocious."

Jack laughed and surrendered the quill.

"Question one," I said as I dipped the quill into the inkpot and wrote the number. "How do you get from Duke Roland's castle to Guy de Trabant's fortress?"

EIGHT

It took three days of making lists, of tossing ideas back and forth, but finally the morning arrived when Jack, Mama, and I stood beside another beanstalk. This one looked slightly different from the first. It was still green and tall. But where the first beanstalk had reminded me of a tree, the second seemed more like a vine. More sinuous and thinner than the first, it seemed to twist and turn into the sky on its way to the World Above. I wondered if the difference was significant. There were five magic beans left now.

The change of seasons had begun in earnest, summer into autumn. Yesterday had been hot and fair, but overnight the temperature dropped. Fog had crept in, spreading its damp white fingers into every nook and cranny of our farm. Beside us, the beanstalk twisted upward, disappearing into the mist.

"You remember what to do?" Jack asked me, as he shouldered his pack.

"I remember," I assured him.

Jack was referring to the very last item we'd added to the list. A plan that called for me to go up the beanstalk.

According to Jack, Sean had estimated it would take about a week on foot to reach Guy de Trabant's fortress. Once Jack and Sean arrived, they would wait for the next court of assizes, which was held in the castle's great hall. Since the sessions took place every other week, with luck, the two boys shouldn't have to wait long.

The irony of one of the magical emblems on our coat of arms being used by Duke Guy to govern his own people wisely while ours remained neglected was a sore point. It was just one of the injustices that could be remedied if Jack was able to steal back the harp.

We'd decided to allow Jack four weeks to travel to de Trabant's castle, see the harp for himself, assess the overall situation, then come back home. If he had not returned within that time, I'd toss a bean over my own shoulder and go up after him.

Mama and I would chop down this beanstalk tomorrow, when we were sure Jack had had plenty of time to reach the World Above. After that, he would literally be cut off from the World Below. But he'd travel with a bean in his pocket, as I would, assuming I had to go. That left two beans to remain with our mother.

"Well," Jack said. "Here I go."

Mama threw her arms around him and held him close. "Good luck," she whispered. "I am proud of you, my son."

She stepped back, and I moved in for a hug of my own. Jack gave me a squeeze so powerful I swore I felt my ribs crack.

"You know," he murmured, for my ears alone, "I almost want you to come after me. You need an adventure of your own. And I'd really like for you to meet Shannon."

"The most beautiful girl you've ever seen," I teased, even as I tightened my hold.

"You'll see what I mean when you meet her, however it happens."

Jack released me and turned to face the beanstalk. Without another word, he walked to the sinuous green trunk, set his foot against it, grasped the leaves firmly with both hands, and began to climb. The last I saw of him was one brown boot-clad foot, disappearing into the clouds.

One week went by, and then another. My mother and I did our best to keep ourselves occupied. We spent several days over the hot stove turning the last of the late harvest fruits and vegetables into preserves or pickles. Mama did piles of mending, while I cleaned out the barn. We worked so hard I almost didn't have time to worry about what was happening to Jack.

Almost. *Almost.* Because the truth was that it was

all a ruse. Mama knew it just as well as I did. Even as our hands flew from one task to another, our minds were fixed on the World Above.

By the middle of the third week, I think both Mama and I knew the truth. Jack was not coming home. This was not to say that something dire had occurred. It might be that it had taken longer to reach de Trabant's fortress than Sean the giant had predicted, which could mean, in turn, that it would take Jack longer to return home. Perhaps Jack had even discovered an unexpected way to get close to the harp and was attempting to get it back.

The trouble was, maybe's and perhaps'es were all Mama and I had. We didn't *know*. And the only way to turn uncertainties into understanding was for me to journey to the World Above.

"It's all my fault," I said at dinner that night, the fear I'd been harboring ever since Jack had vanished up the beanstalk at long last bursting out. "If I hadn't suggested that Jack try to use the wizard's gifts to prove who he was in the first place—"

"No," my mother said firmly. Fear and frustration ran through her voice. "If anything, the fault is mine. I'm the one who filled both your heads with tall tales."

She threw her hands up, the way you do when you concede an argument even though you think you're right.

"I just wanted you to know who you really are," she said. "Is that so wrong?"

"Of course it isn't," I answered at once. "It's just . . ." I paused. "It's not a story anymore, is it? I guess it never really was. Our father really was murdered. If Guy de Trabant could have caught you, there's every chance he would have killed you as well."

"And now," my mother said, "for all we know, Jack may be in the same danger."

"We *don't* know," I replied. "That's the problem." I pushed my plate of food away. I wasn't eating it anyhow. "The good news is that I can remedy that fact." I stood up. "And I should do so."

"I just wish we knew more about this Sean and Shannon," my mother said as she rose in her turn. She went into the kitchen and got down the sugar bowl. "What if they're not as virtuous as they seem? What if they're leading Jack into a trap of some kind?"

"Jack's a pretty good judge of character, Mama," I consoled. "If he thinks we can trust them, my guess is that we can."

"You're right. I know you're right," said my mother. She removed the lid from the sugar bowl. Heads close together, we peered inside. Just four speckled beans remained.

"They look like four wishes," I said softly.

"Perhaps they are," my mother replied. Carefully she tipped one of the beans into my outstretched palm. "That's a rather fanciful notion for you, Gen."

I gave a quick laugh that didn't sound all that convincing, even to my own ears. "Maybe I'm practicing for the World Above."

I closed my hand around the bean. I could feel it, pressing into the center of my palm. "I think I'd like to go to the cornfield by myself, if that's all right."

"Of course it is, sweetheart," said my mother. "Just don't think about it too much. Trust the magic."

"Okay," I said. "I'll try."

"But you're not a tryer, are you?" my mother said. "You're a doer, Gen. I think you have been from the day you were born. I used to think it was your affinity to the World Below, but now I'm not so sure. I think it's just the way you are, and I am glad for it."

"Thank you, Mama," I said, surprised.

My mother bent to kiss my cheek. "Go along now. And remember—don't stop to think too much along the way."

I did my best. Honestly, I did. But all the way to the cornfield, with the bean clutched tightly in my palm, I wondered. If, in my innermost heart of hearts, I still harbored a tiny seed of doubt, would the magic work? Could my attachment to the World Below, which I'd secretly always been so proud of, doom my brother to destruction in the World Above?

You're failing already, Gen, I thought as I reached the cornfield. Since Jack had grown the last beanstalk, our neighbors had come to help us harvest the corn. Jack's absence had been noticed, but not spoken of. I had seen the worry, and the judgment, in the other men's eyes. My mother needed all the help she could get. Where was her son? There was no way to explain. I wondered what the neighbors would think when our family disappeared entirely. If we did. If we didn't, we would face hard times.

I gazed at the cornfield. It looked as bleak as my sudden turn of thought. Where before tall stalks had stood, now there was nothing but stubble. My beanstalk, assuming I could actually get one to grow, would have no camouflage.

There's a lesson in here somewhere, I thought. It was time to see if I could find it. Turning my back to the field, I planted my feet and whispered a quick prayer to whoever might be listening.

Please, I thought. *Let me succeed in spite of myself.*

I let the bean fly. I did not turn to try and see where it landed. I tried to trust the magic, to let it take its course.

Now there was only one thing I could do: wait for morning.

"Well," my mother said the following day. "So much for your concerns."

I had grown a beanstalk all right, a sinewy column of green reaching into the sky. It swayed despite there being no breeze, and looked as if a puff of air might knock it down.

But when I set my hand on the trunk, I felt the beanstalk's inner core of strength. Felt that it possessed a single desire: to carry me and only me from the World Below to the World Above. The fluttering leaves reminded me of waving hands, beckoning me upward.

"You take good care now, Gen," my mother said.

"I will. Don't forget to chop down the beanstalk."

"I'll remember," she said quietly, and I realized that for the first time in sixteen years my mother would be all alone. Alone in the place that had been both her sanctuary and her exile. I opened my mouth to say something, but Mama spoke first.

"I'm proud of you, Gen." At her words I let go of the beanstalk. "I've always been proud of you. I probably haven't said that as much as I should."

My eyes filled with tears, but I did not let them fall. In this, at least, I was my mother's daughter.

"I understand, Mama," I said quietly. Now that I was about to embark on an adventure of my own, a great peace seemed to come over me. "You and Jack are so much more alike. And he's so . . . charming. Don't you dare tell him I said that. If you do, I'll just deny it."

"I wouldn't dream of it," my mother said with the faintest hint of a smile. The kind that caused only one dimple to appear, rather than two. "But I mean it, you know."

"I'm sorry I never really believed," I said. "Not the way Jack did."

"It doesn't make any difference," my mother replied. Her eyes focused on the beanstalk for a moment, then returned to mine. "You believe now. Be safe and smart up there, my Gen. Be yourself."

Before I could answer, she turned away and walked quickly toward the house. I turned to face the beanstalk.

There is no going back now, I thought.

For better or worse, there was only going forward. There was only going *up*. Seizing the trunk of the beanstalk with both hands, I pushed off from the World Below and began to climb.

NINE

How shall I tell you? How shall I even begin to describe what it was like to climb that beanstalk?

It was hard. A lot harder than I thought it would be, and it wasn't just that the climb was long or that my dratted skirts slowed me down. I'd never been one of those girls who longed to do everything the boys did. Why should I? I did most of Jack's chores anyway. But scrambling up that beanstalk hand over hand, hour after hour, I wished I'd had the foresight to put on a pair of pants.

Climbing a beanstalk is not like climbing a tree. A tree trunk is firm and hard. It feels unyielding beneath your feet and hands. Even when the wind moves through its branches, a tree feels solid. You can remind yourself that the tree lives and breathes, just as you do yourself. If you really put your imagination to work, you can conjure up an image of sap flowing, deep within. But it's difficult to really feel this beneath your hands.

From the moment I first touched it, I knew that the beanstalk was different. Never in my life had I felt anything so magical, so alive.

The surface of the stalk was slightly tacky, which helped my hands maintain a firm grip, and kept my feet from slipping as I braced myself. The stalk itself was precisely the right diameter for me. Thick enough so that I could get a good grip, my fingers just touching as I closed my hand around it, but not so thick that my hands grew tired.

Leaves sprang from the stalk with what I can only describe as wild abandon. Some stayed in close, as if huddled against the stalk for protection; others unfurled into the open air, as if eager to explore. But no matter where they were, the leaves never stopped moving. The slightest breath of air made them dance and flutter.

Though I soon found I could rely on its sturdiness and strength (besides, having committed myself, what choice did I have?), it was slightly disconcerting to realize that not just the leaves, but the entire beanstalk itself, was always in motion. It swayed ever so slightly. Whether this was the result of my own movement, or was simply an attribute of all magic beanstalks, I had no way to discover.

I soon found myself settling into a rhythm, grasping a set of leaves with my right hand, boosting myself upward with my right foot braced against the trunk, then repeating the actions on the opposite side. I grew tired. I stopped to catch my breath, leaning my forehead against the great green trunk. My breath my own once more, I recommenced my climb.

Birds fluttered around my head, as if curious about this new creature invading their airy realm. But finally even those dropped away as I continued to climb. Hand over hand, hour after hour, up, up, up, until the very notion of the passage of time lost all meaning. There was only me and the beanstalk. All around us, the wide-open sky, the great expanse between the World Below and the World Above.

I did not look down.

It never even occurred to me to do this, believe it or not. All my energy, all my attention, was focused on going *up*. The higher I climbed, the more filled with possibilities the air seemed to become.

It got cooler too, after a while. Thin wisps of cloud drifted by. Gradually they became more dense, finally coalescing into a cloud so thick I could barely see the beanstalk. I could hear my heart, thundering inside my chest. My breath, whooshing in, puffed out white to become one with the cloud.

Surely I must be almost there, I thought. For what else could this be but the layer of cloud that Mama had always claimed divided the World Above and the World Below?

Reach with the right hand, boost with the right foot. Reach with the left hand, boost with the left foot. *Keep going. Keep going. You can do this, Gen*, I thought.

Jack had done it twice. I'd never prove myself to be my father's daughter if I couldn't even do it once.

As if thinking of my father had been a secret password, my head popped out through the cloud. The sun was so dazzling I squinted my eyes nearly shut. Slowly I eased my right eyelid open, and then the left, blinking rapidly in astonishment.

Oh my, I thought.

I was in the World Above. Or at least my head and shoulders were. The rest of me was still in transition, below the cloud layer.

The new world rested on the surface of the cloud as if the mist was some strange bedrock. *No wonder this is a place where magic happens*, I thought. I pulled myself a little farther up the beanstalk, far enough to rest my elbows on the soil of the World Above. I could see the top of the beanstalk now, waving back and forth as if offering its congratulations.

I looked around. To tell you the absolute truth, the World Above looked an awful lot like the World Below, except for the fact that the ground didn't look quite solid. In places, the land looked as dense and permanent as it was in the World Below. But in others, like around the beanstalk, for example, the cloud showed through, as if revealing a hidden portal.

Then, as I watched, the land shifted, sliding along the layer of cloud. And just like that, nearly all evidence of the cloud was gone.

Stop gawking like a tourist and get a move on, Gen, I thought. I wasn't sure what would happen if the

World Above shifted when I was still half in, half out, but I was absolutely sure I didn't want to find out.

Using the ground itself for leverage, I dug my elbows in and gave myself a boost, pulling my legs up into the World Above. Quickly I rolled away from the beanstalk and lay flat on my back. I lay still for a moment, stretched full length.

I'm here, I thought. *This is real. I am in the World Above.*

For a moment I was dizzy, as if my body could not decide to which world it belonged. I closed my eyes, taking deep, steadying breaths. The air smelled sweet, like honey.

When I opened my eyes, the beanstalk was gone.

All right, that's it, I thought. I scrambled to my feet, filled with determination to be about my mission. *Which way to Father's castle?* I wondered. *How can I find Shannon and Sean?*

As it happened, my questions were answered before I could take so much as a step.

"Well, it's about time," an exasperated voice behind me said. "What took you so long?"

TEN

I spun around. Standing before me, hands on hips, was the most beautiful young woman I had ever seen. A riot of dark curls danced around her face. Her skin was golden, as if from long hours in the sun. She had bright eyes of a color I can only describe as violet. I couldn't quite read the expression in them. Hope, fear, irritation, and curiosity were all crowded in together. She wore a simple countrywoman's garments, just as I did. Sturdy shoes. A dress of brown homespun with an apron over it.

"You're Shannon," I blurted out. Hardly the most brilliant way to start.

"And you're Gen," she responded.

We continued to stare at each other.

"You don't look as much like Jack as I thought you would."

"That's because we're really not that much alike,"

I answered, then bit my tongue. Confessing how different Jack and I were might not be such a good idea, I realized. After all, Shannon and her brother had helped Jack. Liking him had to account for at least part of why they'd done so.

"You, on the other hand, are exactly as Jack described," I said, determined to get it right this time. "He said you were the most beautiful girl he'd ever seen."

"He did not," Shannon protested at once. But her face had flared a bright red. Even as she made her swift denial, I saw the hope leap into her eyes.

So the attraction is mutual, I thought. Had she and Jack fallen in love? What would it feel like to do this so suddenly? To fall in love at first sight?

"He did too," I said with a smile. We sounded like a couple of bickering six-year-olds. "I don't suppose you happen to know where he is."

"Not precisely," Shannon replied, her blush vanishing abruptly. "He and Sean—that's my brother—set out for the de Trabant lands almost a month ago. I don't know what's happened to them, but I'm starting to fear the worst. But you know all this. It's why you've come. Jack said you would, if things went . . . wrong."

"We don't know that anything's wrong," I said forcefully, as if a firm tone would convince us both.

"Why don't you let me take your pack?" Shannon offered. "You must be tired and hungry after your climb. Come up to the house and we can decide what to do next."

The house, of course, was actually a castle, my parents' former home.

"We've done our best to maintain things," Shannon said as we walked. My beanstalk had not been quite as obliging as Jack's when it came to location. It had deposited me a bit farther away from the castle. The farmer in whose field my beanstalk had appeared had been keeping an eye on it, waiting to see who it might bring to the World Above. At the first sight of me, he'd run to fetch Shannon.

"But there are only two of us now," Shannon went on. "Even when our father was alive, it was a lot to take care of. We really only live in the rooms off the kitchen. They're easier to heat in winter, and in summer I'm close to the garden."

"I'm sure you made the right choices," I said. We walked in silence for a moment or two. I kept my eyes focused on the short grass of the path in front of us. When I spoke, I wanted to make sure I said precisely what I meant.

"From what Jack told Mama and me, you and your family put the people of what used to be Duke Roland's kingdom first. No one in our family is going to find fault with that. I'd like to think it's what we would have done ourselves."

I could feel Shannon's eyes on me as we walked along.

"I think I like you," she finally said. "I wasn't sure I would."

I gave a quick laugh. "Well, that's honest. To return

the favor, I wasn't so sure I wanted to come to the World Above. I wasn't sure I believed it existed until Jack grew that first beanstalk."

"I can understand that," Shannon said.

I stopped walking. "*What?*"

"Well, it only stands to reason," she said, coming to a halt in her turn. "Jack said you were the practical one, the one who gets things done. I don't imagine that leaves much time for daydreaming, even if you had the inclination for it."

"It doesn't," I said. "You're absolutely right."

Shannon and I fell into step again. We continued in silence for several moments.

"Do you know that you're the first, the only, person who's ever understood that?" I asked finally. "Don't you think that's ironic? The only person to understand why I never really believed in the World Above is the first person I meet once I get there. So, for the record, I think I like you, too."

Shannon smiled. "That's a pretty good sign. And now we know two things we have in common."

"What's the other one?"

"Being practical," Shannon replied.

We reached the span of a stone bridge, long but so narrow the two of us brushed shoulders as we continued to walk side by side. Beneath us was a deep, wide expanse. Ahead of us was a great building cut from the same stone as the bridge, a somber, cloudy-day gray. But every now and then, as the sun glanced off it, I thought I caught glimpses of different colors running through it. Amber. Silver. Gold. Its towers seemed imposing yet somehow graceful at the same time.

This is it, I thought. This castle had been my parents' home, the one my mother had come to as a bride. The one she'd left to confirm her dearest hope, only to be kept away by Guy de Trabant's coup sixteen years ago.

Oh, Mama! How I wish that you could be here! I swear to you I'll find the way soon, I thought.

"Speaking of practical," I said when I'd finally found my voice, "I assume this bridge is narrow to help keep invaders at bay."

"It is," Shannon said, nodding. I caught the way she turned her head to look at me. I was pretty sure I knew what we were both thinking. In the end, the bridge hadn't done any good. The "invader" who had robbed my father of both his kingdom and his life had had no need to cross it. He was already inside.

"We're crossing what used to be the moat," Shannon went on. "After Guy de Trabant abandoned the castle, the water dried up. I don't know why, but it's turned out all right. The moat bed has some of the best soil in the country."

"So you turned it into a garden," I said, suddenly delighted. I stopped, leaning out to gaze over the side.

"Gardens," Shannon corrected. Now that I had stopped to look closely, I could see that she was right. The moat bed was filled with individual garden plots. Even when they looked to be growing precisely the same things, each was still slightly different from the one beside it. A woman with a bright kerchief on her head looked up and waved. I waved back.

"It looks like a patchwork quilt," I said.

Shannon smiled. "We started by giving everyone in the closest village a plot," she explained, "then expanded to other villages when we discovered we had room enough. When you add what's grown here to what I raise on the castle grounds and what people grow on their own lands, nobody goes hungry. We pool our resources."

"It's a fine idea," I said. "And a fine piece of work. You should be proud." Shannon remained silent, her eyes focused on some point in the distance.

"But it's not the same, is it?" I asked quietly. "It's not the same as being a famous giant. It's not the same as traveling through the countryside being hailed as a hero."

"Not a hero—not exactly," Shannon said quickly. "And that's not why Sean does it, nor Papa before him."

"No," I said. "Of course not. Still, you're the one in your family who's different, aren't you? Just like I'm the one who's different in mine."

"It's silly, really." Shannon shrugged. "I mean, it's not as if I actually *want* to be a giant. Do you have any idea what it takes to make a set of Sean's clothes?"

"No, but I'll bet you do, right down to how many stitches it takes to set in a sleeve or mend a hole in his trousers."

Shannon gave a snort. "It depends on the size of the hole, though as a general rule, think large."

I smiled. "Jack's holes might not be so big, but I bet there were more of them. He got into every kind of scrape imaginable as a boy. Nothing Mama ever said could convince him not to fill his clothes quite so full of holes. Sometimes she couldn't even figure out how they'd got there."

Shannon matched my smile with one of her own. But I saw the way her hands gripped the top of the stone wall until her knuckles turned white. I saw the way the edges of her lips quivered even as she turned them up.

"I bet neither of us would complain about mending again," she said, "if only Sean and Jack would come home."

"We're going to find them," I said, reaching to cover one of her hands with mine. "We're going to find a way, you and I. That's why you send the practical ones in last, the ones who don't care about having an adventure."

I gave her fingers a squeeze, and then let go. "But first I need a nap and something to eat. I hate to sound like a wimp, but I'm exhausted."

"Of course you're tired," Shannon said. "You just climbed a magic beanstalk."

"I did, didn't I?" I said. I gazed over the side of the stone bridge, out into the World Above.

Was the green here more vivid, or was that just my imagination? Was the air filled with sweeter smells?

I tilted my head back to watch a flock of birds as it wheeled across the sky. They were of no kind I recognized.

"I really, really did. I'm still not quite sure how."

"You climbed the beanstalk the same way you do everything else," Shannon said simply.

"By doing it," I replied.

This time she laughed, the sound pure and high. Above our heads, I heard one of the birds call, as if in answer. I felt my heart lift, rising to join the sound.

"Okay, now I *really* like you," Shannon said. And I knew it was because I'd given the same answer she would have herself.

"I'm really glad to hear it," I answered.

Side by side we entered the great stone castle. With enough practice, I thought I just might be able to make it feel like coming home.

ELEVEN

"There's something I've been meaning to ask you," I said some time later. Shannon and I were seated at the wide trestle table in the castle's sunny kitchen. Above our heads, herbs hung upside down to dry on a rack suspended from the ceiling. They gave the room a pungent yet homey smell.

Like Jack, climbing a beanstalk had given me a healthy appetite. The remains of the meal Shannon and I had, including the best bread I'd ever tasted, lay on the table before us.

"What do you want to know?" Shannon asked now.

"Why did you help Jack in the first place?" I asked. "I mean, aside from the—" Suddenly afraid I might give offense, I broke off.

"I think the word you're afraid to say is 'obvious,'" Shannon said with a chuckle.

"I'm sorry. It's really none of my business how you and Jack feel about each other. But he was pretty clear about his feelings for you. What does it feel like to fall in love so suddenly?"

Shannon made a wry face. "Sort of like falling down a hole. The ground beneath you disappears without warning, and your stomach goes right up into your throat."

"I don't think I'll try it," I teased. "It doesn't sound all that pleasant."

"It's not so bad," Shannon said. We smiled at each other. "But we both digress. What was it you really wanted to know?"

"Why you and Sean helped Jack," I replied. "You pretty much had to take him on faith. He had no real way of proving he was who he said he was."

"As a matter of fact, he did," Shannon countered. She got to her feet. "He just didn't know it. Sean and I weren't sure if we should show him this. He had such stars in his eyes about the World Above. But I think it's safe to show you. Come on."

With Shannon in the lead, we left the kitchen and made our way through a wide passage that connected to the main part of the house. *What must this have been like when my parents lived here?* I wondered. Men and women dressed in their finest to attend a state banquet or a ball. Servants bustling back and forth, staggering under the weight of trays laden with food and drink. The rooms through which I walked were cold and silent now. But once they would have been filled with the sounds of laughter, the whispers of court intrigue. They had been filled with life.

"My mother never talks about her life here," I murmured. "Except for the bedtime stories she used to tell us." *And I never asked her about it,* I thought.

"Is that so surprising?" Shannon asked. We ascended a flight of stairs, our feet slapping softly against the stones. "Everyone talks about how happy the duke and duchess were, even after all this time. There are still old folks who can remember your parents' wedding. They tell the stories with tears in their eyes, not just out of sorrow, but also out of joy. Maybe your mother's memories make her feel both things at once too."

"Perhaps they do," I acknowledged quietly. Why had I not considered this possibility before? *How could you have, Gen?* I thought. *You never truly believed in the World Above.*

"I think my mother's always felt a little guilty," I went on slowly, as if feeling my way along. "Guilty that she wasn't here that night. Though if she had been, it's likely she'd have been killed as well. And Jack and me too, of course."

"So you see her problem," Shannon said with a nod.

"I believe I do," I said.

"This way," Shannon said. "It's not much farther now." She gestured at the space around us. "This is the old great hall."

I gave a quick laugh in spite of myself. "I should think so."

A huge vaulted stone ceiling soared above our heads. Cut-glass windows cast a pattern of rainbows onto the floor. There was a broad central stair and narrower hallways leading I-had-no-idea-where on either side.

"It was old Bertrand, the stable master, who found this," Shannon explained. She opened the first door along the passage and went into the room beyond. I followed.

"He said it was buried under a pile of hay in one of the stalls. Many of the duke's servants were still living when we first came here, and they were slow to trust us. To this day, no one has come forward to claim saving what I'm about to show you. Please wait here, by the door."

Obeying her instructions, I paused while Shannon entered the room. From where I stood, I could see it was filled with what I assumed were pieces of furniture swathed in muslin. Shannon walked to the far side of the room and turned an object around. Then she drew aside the piece of muslin and stepped away.

I caught my breath. It was a painting of a man and woman.

Mama! I thought.

For the young woman in the painting could be no one but my mother. There was her long, golden hair and her cornflower blue eyes. And there were the dimples in her cheeks as she smiled up at the man at her side.

Duke Roland, I thought as I gazed at the face of my father for the very first time.

Duke Roland had a strong face. His chin was square and determined. He had a firm mouth, even when curved in a smile. He gazed from out of his portrait with clear gray eyes. Slowly, my feet whispering against the stone floor, I moved until I was directly before the portrait. My parents stood close together, their bodies touching. My father had one arm wrapped around my mother's waist. Her head tilted back to rest against his shoulder.

Oh, look! I thought. *See how much they loved each other.*

No wonder coming to the World Below had felt like exile to my mother. I didn't realize I was weeping until Shannon spoke.

"I'm sorry," she said. "Perhaps I should not have shown you."

"No," I said at once. I shook my head and felt the tears fly. "I'm glad you did. But I think you're right. This would have been too much for Jack, at least right off. One glimpse of this, and he'd have set off to avenge our father."

Except for the color of his eyes, Jack was the image of Duke Roland.

The shape of their faces was precisely the same. In the curve of Duke Roland's lips, I saw the curve of Jack's mouth when he smiled. Jack had our father's wide, sweeping cheekbones, the almond shape of his eyes. But while Jack's eyes were blue like our mother's,

Duke Roland's were as gray as storm clouds.

"This must be hard for you, too," Shannon said softly. "You look so much like her."

My head turned toward her as if pulled by a string. "What?"

"Surely you can see the resemblance," she said. She moved to stand beside me. "You look as much like her as Jack looks like your father." She cocked her head to one side. "Though, if it's not presumptuous of me to say so, I think I can see your father in you as well. Something about the determined set of the chin, I think."

"I wish I'd known him," I said softly. "And I wish I'd taken time to know my mother."

"At least you can do something about the second," Shannon said. I felt a sudden burst of affection sweep over me for this girl I barely knew. Not only had it been the right thing to say, it had been the right way to say it, simple and straightforward. Practical, just as I was myself.

She is right, I thought. I could still get to know my mother better. And hadn't Mama said I had my father's nature? My ability to plan, my single-mindedness when it came to getting a job done. I was Duke Roland's child. I was his heir, his firstborn. Who knew what I might discover if I stopped comparing myself to Jack and simply tried to know my own self better?

Jack, I thought.

"We have to find our brothers first," I said.

"Thank you," Shannon said quietly.

I turned back toward her in surprise. "For what?"

"For not saying 'save,'" she said. "Even though it's what we're both thinking."

"What I'm thinking is that we'll do whatever it takes," I said.

With gentle fingers, I reached to cover my parents' portrait.

TWELVE

"I've been thinking it over, and I've decided we should take the shortcut," Shannon announced early the next morning.

We had talked far into the night, trying to determine the best way to locate our brothers. We would head for Guy de Trabant's fortress, of course. But unlike Jack and Sean, we would go on horseback, though even that would take time. Shannon estimated five full days. What if Jack and Sean needed help *now*?

Perhaps it had been seeing the portrait of my parents, or seeing how much Jack looked like our father, but a sense of urgency now seized me and would not let go. I had tossed and turned as I slept, anxious and edgy. My skin crawled with impatience. I had already waited nearly four whole weeks before following Jack to the World Above. Traveling another five days before I could learn about my brother's fate seemed . . . wrong. Even worse, it seemed dangerous.

Too long. The thought pounded in my head to the rhythm of my heart. *Too long. Too long.*

"What's the shortcut?" I inquired.

We were in the stables, readying the castle's one remaining horse. Even in my haste to be gone, I eyed him dubiously. He was ancient and swaybacked. Surely there was no way he could carry us both. But Shannon had assured me that, like the rest of my father's subjects, the old horse would prove steadfast and loyal. His name, as a matter of fact, was Verité. Truth. Appropriate, there was no denying it. Shannon tossed a blanket across Verité's broad back, then added our saddlebags before she replied.

"Through the Greenwood Forest."

I caught my breath. "But I thought you said . . ." My voice trailed off.

"I did," Shannon answered. "I know. But I still think it's the right choice."

The Greenwood lay like a great green divide between de Trabant's lands and ours. The boundary that marked the place where our lands had once ended and Duke Guy's began was somewhere deep inside the Greenwood itself, Shannon said, though she had never seen it. The place was marked by an ancient oak. My mother had grown up not far from the Greenwood. Rowan, her nurse, had built her house along its outskirts, though she, and it, had vanished long ago.

As Rowan herself had predicted, it hadn't taken

Guy de Trabant long to figure out where my mother had gone. But by the time his soldiers reached the wise old woman's cottage, neither Rowan nor my mother were anywhere to be found. When word of my mother's escape reached Guy de Trabant, he'd flown into a rage and ordered Rowan's house burned to the ground. No one had seen her since.

With Rowan's departure, a change had come over the Greenwood, or so the local inhabitants told. Where once it had been safe for travelers to pass, outlaws now made the forest their home. One was of particular note: Robert de Trabant, Guy de Trabant's only son.

"Going through the Greenwood could save us as many as three days," Shannon continued. "I know it's risky, but I think it's a chance worth taking. Surely not every tree harbors a ruffian. They say the duke's son and his band stay mostly near the border with the kingdom of Larienne."

I had never heard of Larienne before, and said so. "I have never seen it myself," Shannon told me. "But it's rumored to be so wealthy that the merchants line their bathtubs with gold tiles."

I gestured at our country garments. "We're not wealthy, that much is obvious."

"Precisely," Shannon said with a nod. "So there's no real reason for Robert de Trabant and his band to take an interest in us, even if we encounter them. With any luck, though, we'll slip through quietly with no one the wiser."

I hesitated for a moment, my fingers fiddling with Verité's long mane. "I hate to say this," I finally said. "But I don't think relying on luck is a very good plan."

Shannon gave a short bark of unamused laughter. "Don't I know it? But our only other choice is to follow Sean and Jack's example and bypass the forest entirely. I just don't want to take that much time to go around it."

"Nor do I."

"We're agreed then?" Shannon asked. "We go through the Greenwood, even if it is the more dangerous choice."

"We go through the Greenwood." I nodded. "Though I reserve the same right Jack always did."

"What's that?"

"The right to say 'I told you so' if anything goes wrong."

We rode all that day at a steady, even pace that took us through the countryside once governed by my father and mother. Everyone recognized Shannon, and it was clear that the people adored her. In every village or hamlet, the men and women stopped their work and came to greet us. Shannon introduced me simply as her friend Gen. Neither of us offered any additional information.

The women bobbed quick, shy curtsies, their glances fluttering up like butterflies to rest on my face, then back down to rest on the ground. The men doffed their caps, then stood turning them in their hands.

Hope. There is still so much hope here, I thought.

"Do you think they know who I am?" I asked, as we left the farms behind. We were in open country now. Dead ahead, stretching along the horizon in either direction as far as I could see, lay the dark green smudge of the Greenwood.

"Do you suppose Sean and Jack attracted as much attention as we did?"

Did Jack come to feel as I do now? I wondered. Had the people of this place found a way inside his heart? Without knowing a single one of their names, did he feel responsible for them?

"The answer to the second question is most certainly yes," Shannon replied. "Everyone loves Sean. Even the children stop their games when he comes along. As for knowing who you are ... The older ones must suspect, I think; the resemblance to your parents is so strong. But you have to remember that no one here really knows what happened to Duke Roland's young wife. They don't know you and Jack were ever born."

We rode in silence for several moments, the wind shushing through the tall grass and the *thunk* of Verité's hooves against the earth the only sounds.

"It's not what I expected," I finally said. "This country is poor. That much is obvious. But the people seem—" I broke off, frustrated by my inability to explain my impressions. "They don't seem unhappy.

They don't seem desperate or ready to fight with one another at a moment's notice.

"When Jack first returned from the World Above—when he brought back the sickly goose and a nearly empty sack that should have been overflowing with gold—my mother was beside herself. She said it was a sign that the people were not being governed wisely or well. That they were suffering."

"The first part is certainly true," Shannon answered. "As to the second . . ."

She thought a moment before going on. "I think the people miss having a leader," she finally continued. "Someone to look up to, whose protection we can invoke, even if it's only when we tuck our children into bed at night. It's good to be able to put your trust in something greater than yourself. It makes the world less frightening.

"Some nights, many nights, we may worry about the future. We lie in our beds and listen to the wind howl. But when we finally do fall asleep, our dreams are not disturbed by the fear that those we trust will suddenly decide to turn on us. Call it Guy de Trabant's legacy, though I doubt it's one he intended to bestow. The people of this land work together; we look out for one another. We have learned that our survival depends on it."

"We," I said. "You are one of them, not an outsider."

"Of course I'm one of them," Shannon answered simply. "Sean and I haven't been outsiders from the moment the people first realized they could trust

Papa, that he meant to aid them, not bring more harm. Belonging is more than just an accident of birth."

"True enough," I replied.

We rode on. I watched the Greenwood looming ever closer.

"Tell me more about Guy de Trabant's son," I said.

"I don't know all that much," Shannon admitted with a shrug. "His mother died when he was a small child. After that, they say his father tried to keep him close, that having inflicted harm on others, Guy de Trabant was desperate to keep his son from harm at any cost. But Robert de Trabant could not be contained. He was wild. He didn't want to stay inside his father's fortress. He wanted to see the world."

"To have adventures," I murmured.

"Perhaps," Shannon replied. "Whatever his motivation, he was forever slipping away. It didn't matter how many guards his father posted. He mingled with the common people and won their hearts. But when murmurings began that Robert would make a better ruler than his father, Guy de Trabant decided things had gone on long enough.

"He sent his soldiers into the city. They took people from their homes. The women and children were thrown into prison. Able-bodied men and boys were sent to the north, to work in the mines. Duke Guy issued a proclamation. The raids would continue, every week, for as long as his son defied him. When the defiance ceased, so would the people's punishment. But Robert de Trabant would not be cowed. He escaped for good that very night."

"And his father's people?" I asked.

"Safe," Shannon replied. "Or as safe as they can be, considering who sits on their country's throne. Robert de Trabant knew his father better than his father knew himself, or so it seems. Robert called his father's bluff. The persecutions ceased, but Robert de Trabant still has not come home. He's lived in the forest for nearly a year now."

"Where he preys on others by stealing from them," I pointed out. "How does that make him better than his father?"

"They say he steals only from those who would make his father and his nobles rich," Shannon answered. "Even richer than they already are. Robert's a thief, true enough, but what he steals he gives to those who need it most. We've even seen a sack or two of gold or goods appear on the edge of the Greenwood from time to time. Robert de Trabant is like his father in one way, at least. He does not venture far into the territory that once belonged to Duke Roland."

"Let us hope we do not meet him," I said.

Shannon nodded. "Either way, we'll find out soon enough."

She brought Verité to a halt. Our conversation had carried us across the breadth of the meadow to the edge of Greenwood Forest.

We entered it just as the long shadows of late afternoon began to fall.

Thirteen

The setting of the sun made the Greenwood a beautiful, but eerie, place. A strange green and golden light shone around us. The forest itself was silent. The voices of the day birds had ceased; night birds had not yet commenced their calls. The floor of the forest was a thick carpet of pine needles and dead leaves. Verité's big hooves made hardly any sound as he plodded along.

This place feels old, I thought. Much older than the forest that covered the hills near our farm in the World Below. The trees through which Shannon and I now traveled had enormous trunks, many too large to see around. Their boughs were as curved as Verité's back, as if they'd grown tired of holding themselves upright. Even the pine needles extended downward, brushing against the tops of our heads from time to time as we passed beneath them.

This is a place with secrets, I thought. *It keeps them well.*

The light was fading quickly now. Then, as if a candle had been snuffed out, the sun slipped from sight. The forest was plunged into gloom. A quick chill ran down my spine.

We are going to have to spend the night in this place, I thought, and wondered why I had not considered this before.

"I think we should get down and lead the horse," Shannon said. "We don't want to risk one of us falling off."

"Whatever you say," I agreed.

Shannon swung one leg over Verité's head, and then dropped lightly to the ground. I had my leg halfway across his broad rump when a sound broke the forest's silence.

"What do you suppose we have here, my friends?" asked a playful voice.

Startled, I twisted in the direction of the sound, lost my grip on the horse, and tumbled to the ground.

"Not graceful young noblewomen. You can be sure of that," a second replied.

"Of course we're not noble born," Shannon's sharp tone cut across the laughter that seemed to erupt from all around us.

It's coming from above! I realized. *They are in the trees!*

Shannon helped me to my feet. "Follow my lead," she whispered urgently. I gave a quick nod.

"You can tell we're not noble just by looking at us,"

she continued in a loud voice. "Or don't you care to use your eyes?"

"Oh, we care to use them all right, damsel," the first voice spoke once more.

Not five paces ahead a branch dipped down, and suddenly a young man not much older than Shannon and me was standing on the path in front of us. He was dressed in a strange patchwork of myriad shades of green, the perfect camouflage for the forest. Legs apart, hands on hips, precisely like an adventurer out of one of my mother's bedtime stories. Jack had spent much of his childhood trying to perfect that very stance.

"And we like to use our heads, as well."

"I should certainly hope so," I spoke up firmly despite the way my heart had begun to pound. Shannon had showed no fear. I needed to match her example. "Considering there's likely a price on every single one of them."

"The lass talks sense," the second voice sounded. There was another flurry of branches, and another figure dropped to the ground. "Even if she can't ride a horse."

In the fading light, I could see that this man was older than his companion. If not for the fact that I suspected the younger must be Robert de Trabant, the two might have been father and son.

"Now, Steel," the young man said, his tone mock severe. "That's unfair, and you know it. She was *riding* just fine. It was getting *off* the horse that posed the problem."

Again, a burst of low laughter sounded from the

trees. The young man made a gesture, and at this signal, the rest of his companions began dropping to the ground all around us. Almost before I realized what was happening, Shannon and I were standing in the center of a circle of green-and-brown-clad figures, each no more than an arm's reach from his neighbor. The young man who had appeared first stood facing us. His older companion was at our backs. We were completely surrounded.

"Ladies," the younger man said. He bent low in a bow. "Welcome to Greenwood Forest. What business brings you beneath its boughs?"

Shannon stuck out her chin. "What right do you have to ask us that?" she demanded. "No one owns the forest, as far as I know."

"True enough," the young man acknowledged, but though his words were cordial, his voice was sharp as the edge of a knife. He broke the circle to take several steps toward us, as if to get a better look at who was brave enough to deal with him so boldly.

His hair was a burnished brown, like the skin of a hazelnut, and his eyes were chestnut dark. There was something about them that made me want to gaze right back and look away at the same time. I felt a different sort of shiver move down my spine.

"Most who meet us, however," he continued, his tone conversational, as if discussing the weather, "discover they prefer to share a little something. If not your business, make another choice. But make no mistake: You *will* choose something."

It is you who are making the mistake, I thought. *We may be two girls alone, but we are not so easily browbeaten.*

"We have food and blankets, which we will gladly share with anyone who needs them," I answered, careful to keep my own tone pleasant and mild. "Whatever is in our saddlebags is at your disposal. But if you were hoping for gold or jewels, you're in for a disappointment."

I never had the chance to find out what his response might have been, for as I turned toward Verité to slide the saddlebags from his back, the young man's older companion abruptly darted forward.

"Who are you?" he demanded in a harsh, fierce voice. He grabbed me by the shoulders, thrusting his face directly into mine. "What is your name? From whence do you come?"

"Gen. My name is Gen," I repeated, and felt a surge of pride that my voice sounded strong. Not high and tight, like the band of fear that was wrapping itself around my chest, threatening to cut off my ability to breathe.

"That tells me nothing. Nothing at all." As suddenly as he'd seized me, the man let go. I staggered back, then regained my balance. "Light a torch," he instructed. "I must have more light."

"No," the young man countered swiftly. "It's not safe. We're still too close to the edge of the forest. A light here could be seen through the trees." He moved to stand beside his friend. Both of them gazed at me in the gathering dark.

"What is it, Steel?" the youth asked softly. "Tell me what you see, and what you fear."

"It isn't what I fear, young Robin," replied the man named Steel. "I set aside fear a long time ago. The thing that troubles me now is what I hope."

"Hope," Robin echoed. "That is a word I've not heard in quite some time, and then only . . ."

There was a beat of silence. Then he bowed once more, with genuine respect this time.

"Ladies, you are to be our guests. Please accept our escort through Greenwood Forest."

FOURTEEN

As soon as the decision that we would accompany the band had been made, Robin began to issue a series of orders in a clear, low voice.

This must be Robert de Trabant, I thought. For the others obeyed him without question, moving to do his will at once. Several members broke off from the band to walk ahead as scouts. The rest of us left the path and set off two abreast, walking as swiftly as the diminishing light allowed.

We're in for it now, I thought. I didn't think Shannon knew her way through the forest, aside from following the path, and I most certainly did not. We were now completely at the mercy of Robin de Trabant and his band of thieves. I tried to console myself by thinking that if they'd intended to harm Shannon and me, surely they'd have done so by now.

But they still don't know who I really am, I thought.

Robin now took the lead, with Shannon at his side. Steel and I followed, with the rest of the band at regular intervals behind. Last of all was a single man leading Verité.

How silently they move! I thought. Sure-footed, even in the gathering dark. My own feet felt clumsy by comparison, my body tired and slow, as if the stress of my journey was suddenly catching up with me. Had it really only been two nights ago that I'd slept soundly in my own bed in the World Below?

As if in answer, my toe caught on an unseen tree root. I managed to stifle a cry, but only Steel's quick grip on my elbow saved me from pitching forward onto my face.

"Thank you," I said when I was steady on my feet once more. "I'm not usually this clumsy."

There was a moment's silence, stretching just long enough that I began to fear that Steel would not reply. *Should I try to fill the silence?* I wondered. *Why does this man care who I am?*

"You are more than welcome," he finally said. "You must be very tired."

Be careful. Watch your words as well as your steps, my mind warned. He'd made a simple statement, but there were questions hidden in it, traps for the unsuspecting. *Why are you so tired? How far have you come?*

"Steel is an unusual name," I observed instead. "Do they call you that for the quickness of your hands or of your mind?"

I felt rather than saw the way his head turned

toward me, but it was not yet so dark that I could not see the flash of white teeth as he smiled.

"I think it is your mind that is the quick one, mistress," he replied. "But to answer your question, all of us leave our former names behind when we choose to live in this place."

"For your skill with a blade, perhaps," I suggested.

"Something like that," he answered. The tone of his voice told me the conversation was over. Though my feet stayed steady, Steel reached to guide me by the elbow as the path began to climb abruptly. "Not much farther now."

We topped the rise. Below me, at the bottom of the slope, I could see a cluster of tents, each beside a flickering campfire. The air felt cooler, and I heard the sound of running water. Robin de Trabant's camp was spread along its shores, protected by the high embankments on either side.

They are well hidden, I thought.

"Come down," Steel said. "There is food, and you'll be able to rest."

And there is light, and you'll be able to see my face more clearly, I thought.

"Thank you," I said. "You are very kind."

Steel squeezed my elbow, bringing us both to a halt.

"I am many things, Mistress Gen," he said in a quiet voice. "I'm not sure kind is one of them, not for many years now."

"Surely others are the best judge of that," I answered

steadily, though I could feel my heart begin to pound. Why did this man always seem to be fencing words with me? Why would he not say what was on his mind?

"Perhaps they are," Steel said. "Let us see what judgment you make before the night is out."

Together we walked down the slope toward the light of the campfires.

The camp was larger than it first appeared. Additional tents were clustered just beyond a nearby bend in the river. Robin and Steel received a warm, though subdued, welcome.

How careful they all are, even in their joy, I thought.

Either the appearance of newcomers was so commonplace it no longer caused a stir, or the respect Robin's people had for him kept their curiosity at bay. I had a feeling it was a combination of both. Shannon and I were silent as we traversed the camp.

Robin settled us at a tent and campfire a short distance from the main group. Secretly, I suspected he'd just relinquished his own lodging for the night. Then he disappeared into the darkness with Steel at his side. Shannon and I stood looking at each other.

"Well, so much for getting through the forest undetected," Shannon remarked. She plopped down on a broad, flat rock near the campfire. Abruptly exhausted, I sat down beside her. In the fire's flickering light, I could see the tension etched across my new friend's features.

"What do you suppose will happen to us now?"

I asked in a whisper. The nearest tent was about a stone's throw away, far enough so that we wouldn't be easily overheard; but sounds can carry farther than one expects.

"Steel knows who I am, or at least he suspects. I can think of several reasons for that, most of them not very comforting."

I twisted my neck, trying to take in our surroundings, which was all but impossible in the dark.

"I don't suppose it will do us any good to try and make a run for it," I went on.

"And go in which direction?" Shannon asked. She shook her head. "No. If nothing else, I think we must wait till morning. Then perhaps we can appeal to Robin's better instincts, assuming that he has some."

"He must be Robert de Trabant, don't you think?" I asked. I leaned in close, my voice barely audible.

Shannon nodded. "It makes sense," she agreed. "Robin is a common enough nickname for Robert. And the people here all seem to defer to him."

"They do more than that," I said. "Even from the little we've seen, I can tell they clearly have great affection for him. That still doesn't tell us what he's going to do with us. Particularly once he finds out who I really am."

Shannon reached over and squeezed my hand. "There's no reason to assume the worst," she said.

"You think not? Robin is still Guy de Trabant's son. Currently he's heir to two kingdoms combined. But if I can prove my family's claim, he's back down to one. Even the runaway son of a duke might have something to say about that."

"A runaway son with a price on his head," Shannon told me. "Put there by his father. And something tells me we'll know Robin's intentions soon enough. He doesn't strike me as the type to keep things to himself for long."

"I beg your pardon," a voice cut through our conversation. I looked up. A figure stood just outside the circle of firelight. "Robin said I was to return these to you, with his compliments."

A boy took a step forward into the light, holding our saddlebags out in front of him.

"Thank you," I said, speaking in my normal tone. I gave Shannon's hand a squeeze, then stood. I took the saddlebags from the boy, then carried them back to my place by the fire and set them on a rock. The boy hesitated, as if torn between caution and curiosity.

"We have fruit and cheese, a little meat, and some bread," I said, giving in to a sudden impulse. Perhaps the way to allay my own fears was to make another welcome. "We do not have enough for all, but we would be happy to share with those who need it most, if you will show us who they are."

"You have bread?" the boy asked, his eyes wide. "Real bread, not the flat stuff, baked on a stone?"

Shannon gave an unexpected chuckle. "Real bread," she affirmed. She got up and opened the saddlebag closest to her. "Baked in a brick oven just this morning. But my friend is right. We have just two loaves, and that is not enough for everyone. We are strangers and do not know the way you decide things among you."

She removed a loaf from the saddlebag and held it up. "Will someone help us?" she asked in a voice meant to be heard throughout the camp.

There was a moment's silence. I could almost feel the people around us weighing the situation, making up their minds.

"Mad Tom and his wife have a child who is ill," a woman's voice finally called back.

"Mad Tom?" I echoed.

The boy at our fire nodded. "On account of the way he never loses his temper," he explained, as if I should have been able to figure that out for myself.

I smiled. "Of course."

From out of the shadows, a woman materialized beside the boy.

"They've had a hard time getting the child to eat," she explained, and I recognized her voice. She was the one who had spoken on behalf of Mad Tom's family. "But I have some broth. If they had some bread, they could dip that in it. It's nourishing. I bet the boy would eat that right down."

"They must have some bread then," Shannon said with a nod. "Who else would you suggest? May I please borrow a knife? Someone seems to have appropriated mine."

"I've a knife you can borrow," a voice offered. A man with ginger whiskers stepped into the circle of firelight. He took a knife from a sheath at his belt and extended it, hilt first, toward Shannon. She accepted it and began to carve the first loaf. Before long, our campfire was host to a serious yet friendly crowd.

The discussion of how to divide the bread was sometimes heated, but no one took offense if his or her suggestion was overruled. Shannon didn't touch the knife to the bread until each decision had been agreed on by all involved. Those whose suggestions had been approved carried the pieces to the recipients. There was not a doubt in my mind that each piece would make it safely to those who had been chosen to receive the gift. Like the people of my father's former land, these folks had learned the benefits of working together.

Finally two slices of bread remained, the heels from either end of the second loaf.

"If you all agree, I would like one piece to go to this man, to thank him for the loan of his knife," Shannon proposed.

There was a murmur of assent. The man's face turned as red as his hair. Shannon gave him the bread and thanked him.

"What do you say to giving this lad the other piece?" I inquired. "He returned the saddlebags to us. Without him, there would have been no bread to share."

The boy grinned so that I feared his jaw might crack. But to my surprise, instead of reaching for the bread, he put his hands behind his back, shaking his head in denial.

"No, mistress," he said. "By your leave, that isn't right. I only did what Robin asked, and if I take that piece, then you and your friend have none."

I glanced at Shannon. She gave a quick nod.

"We would like you to have it," I told the boy. "In thanks for a job well done."

"You go ahead and take it, Trip," a woman urged.

"That's right, Trip," others echoed. "Go on."

"Trip," I said. "That's what you're called?"

The boy's grin turned sheepish. "On account of the way I'm always falling down."

I laughed before I could help myself. "In that case, we have something in common. I met your Robin by falling off a horse."

"No!" Trip exclaimed in disbelief.

"As a matter of fact, she did," a now familiar voice replied. Robin de Trabant stepped into the firelight with Steel at his side. "But to tell you the truth, it wasn't her fault. I took her by surprise."

"Not you, Robin," the boy named Trip teased, then blushed bright red.

Robin reached out and ruffled the lad's hair, but his eyes stayed on mine. Their color was still the same, of course, but the expression in them was different. They looked puzzled, as if the scene that he'd just witnessed did not match the one he'd expected to see.

"It's true. I took unfair advantage, I admit. The

lady is offering you a gift, young Trip. If I were in your shoes, I'd think twice about saying no."

"Do you really mean for me to have it?" he asked.

"I really do," I said. I took it from Shannon and held it out to the boy.

"Oh, thank you," Trip breathed. "I haven't had real bread in ever so long."

Carefully he cradled the bread between both hands, as if it were gold. Then he took two steps back, spun on his heel, and was gone. As if his departure had been a signal, the others began to fade away. Soon only Robin, Steel, Shannon, and I stood in the circle cast by the light of our campfire. The bandit leader and the older man stood on one side. Shannon and I stood on the other.

Now we'll come to things, I thought.

"That was thoughtfully done," Robin said. He took a stick and began to poke at the fire, gazing into the flames. "Still, you might have kept something for yourselves."

"You suggested we share. We took your suggestion," Shannon answered, matching his casual tone. She cocked her head to one side, like a bird studying a worm. "Though somehow I have the feeling that if we had kept something back, you'd still be dissatisfied. And it was Gen's idea, if you'll recall."

"So it was," Robin acknowledged. With the appearance of perfect unconcern, he stabbed at the coals. "If you were seeking to create some advantage, I'm afraid you'll have to work a little harder than that. These people may not have much, but they are not bribed as easily as that."

The warmth I'd felt at Robin's banter with the boy vanished as hot fury took its place. I took a step closer to him, heedless of the way my skirts came perilously close to the fire.

"You," I said, "are petty, suspicious, and insufferable. I'm surprised these people follow you at all. I guess there must be more to you than meets the eye. Try opening yours."

Robin's head snapped up. "My eyes work just fine, thank you," he said. "It's interpreting what they see that is the challenge. Appearances can be deceptive, after all. The eyes can be fooled by what the heart desires."

"But first," I said, "you must have one."

"Oh, I have a heart," Robin said. "And it's more caring than you know. It would spare an old friend pain, for example. If it could."

"It can't," Steel put in before I could respond. Even through my annoyance, I could hear his tension. "Just let me ask. Let me hear the truth. That's all I want."

"But will she speak the truth?" Robin inquired.

"How dare you?" I said as the heat of my fury abruptly metamorphosed into solid ice. "You don't know me at all. How dare you doubt me? Of course I'll speak the truth."

"Ask your question, Steel," Robin said softly. Even through the cold of my anger, I shivered at the sound of his voice.

"Who are you?" Steel asked, just as he had before. "Your full name, please. That's all I ask."

Now that the moment to declare myself had come, I felt absolutely calm. "My name is Gentian des Jardins," I said in a steady voice. "Gen, for short."

Jack was right, I thought. *Sooner or later, you have to risk yourself.*

"My mother is Celine Marchand," I went on. "My father was Duke Roland des Jardins, murdered and deposed these sixteen years ago. There," I said to the young man I had every reason to believe was Guy de Trabant's son. "Is that truth enough for you?"

Robin did not respond. Instead there was a silence so complete I swear that even the voice of the wind stopped talking. Slowly Steel sank to his knees, head bowed.

"I knew it," he whispered in a tortured voice. "I knew it must be so. You look so much like your mother there could be no other explanation."

He lifted his face, and I could see tears running down his cheeks. "But how is this possible? No trace of Duchess Celine was ever found."

"We have been in hiding," I answered. "Though my mother would have used the word 'exile.'"

"Where?" Robin's voice was like the flick of a whip. "Where can you have been so well hidden that no one in all this land knew your whereabouts?"

"You have answered the question yourself," I said, and watched as his eyes grew wide.

"Merciful heavens," he said. "The World Below."

"I have answered your questions truthfully," I said. "I have given you my name, now give me yours."

"My name is Robert de Trabant," Robin said. "Sixteen years ago my father brought about the death of yours, though he did not strike the blow himself."

A hot white light exploded inside my head. "You can't know that!" I cried out, all sense of caution forgotten. "You weren't there. How can you say that when you can't possibly know?"

"Because he knows I can," Steel replied. He got to his feet slowly, as if his body pained him. "Earlier you asked if I was called Steel because of my quickness with a blade. The truth is that it's just the opposite. Sixteen years ago I wasn't quick or clever enough with my sword. Duke Roland died because of it."

"For mercy's sake," Robin said, and for the first time I heard true passion in his voice. "How many times must we go over the same thing? You were barely a man. You can't keep blaming yourself for—"

Without warning, he stopped. In the sudden stillness, I heard an owl hoot four times, cease, then hoot four times more.

"The scouts you sent out two days ago have returned," Steel said. "That is Slowpoke's call."

"Slowpoke?" I said before I could stop myself. "Wait, don't tell me." Robin's people's nicknames came in two varieties: those that were accurate descriptions of a trait, such as Trip, or those that were opposites, such as Mad Tom. But surely calling a scout Slowpoke could mean only one thing.

"It's because he's the fastest runner."

Robin flashed a smile. Like the pain that had preceded it, this show of emotion was genuine and unguarded. I felt my own lips curving in answer even as my heart performed a strange and sudden lurch inside my chest.

Oh, wait, I thought. *Oh no.*

"You catch on," Robin said. He turned to Steel. "Bring him," he said simply. Steel spun and was gone.

"Are you expecting trouble?" Shannon asked.

"Always," Robin answered. "Mostly from my father's soldiers."

"Your father hunts you like a common outlaw?" I exclaimed.

"Why wouldn't he?" Robin asked bitterly. "It's what I've become. Here they are."

Steel reappeared, accompanied by a man somewhere between his age and Robin's. He was breathing hard.

"How far are they?" Robin asked at once.

Slowpoke sucked in a deep breath before he spoke. "At the Boundary Oak."

FIFTEEN

Steel swore an oath.

"What?" I asked. "What is the Boundary Oak?"

"The marker for the boundary between what used to be your father's lands and mine," Robin replied. He placed a hand on Slowpoke's shoulder, urging him to sit. Gratefully the scout sank down beside the fire. The rest of us remained on our feet. Shannon produced one of our waterskins and pressed it into the scout's hands.

"Please, drink this," she urged.

"Thank you," Slowpoke said quietly. He drank deeply as Robin continued.

"I've heard it said that the tree was planted by the founders of the houses of des Jardins and de Trabant as a token of eternal goodwill and trust. Determined as he is to hunt me down, my father has never sent soldiers beyond the Boundary Oak.

Something must have happened. I wonder what."

"The duke's men were definitely fired up about something," Slowpoke said. He handed the waterskin back to Shannon with a smile. "But I couldn't get close enough to find out why. I'm sorry, Robin. Perhaps I should have tried harder."

"You brought word of their presence swiftly," Robin reassured him. "That is more than enough. Must we break camp tonight, do you think?"

Slowpoke shook his head.

"The soldiers are excited and full of themselves. And they make so much noise that even Trip could hear them coming and still have time to hide. I think there is no need tonight."

"I'm glad to hear that," Robin said. "Thank you for your counsel. We'll break camp at first light. Will you help Steel pass the word?"

Slowpoke got to his feet. "I will, Robin."

"And be sure to get yourself some food," Robin said. He clapped the other man on the shoulder. "Good work. I'll not forget it."

As quickly as they had appeared, Steel and the scout vanished into the night, leaving Shannon and me alone with Robin.

"I know it may not be your first choice," he said. "But I think it will be safest for you to remain with us. You don't want to encounter a group of my father's soldiers on your own."

He hesitated then, the first time I'd seen him do so. "I would like to ask you something, if I may."

He is treating us as equals, I thought. I nodded my assent. As if I'd issued an invitation, Robin crouched down beside the fire. Only after Shannon and I were seated ourselves did I realize I'd just invited Robin to sit at his own campfire.

"Is there any way my father could know about you?" Robin asked. "Any way that he could know you're here in the World Above?"

"About me, no," I said. "But . . ." I paused and turned my head to look at Shannon.

"It's all right," she said. "Tell him."

"I have a brother," I said. "A twin named Jack. He came to the World Above nearly four weeks ago. He was trying to make his way to your father's fortress with Shannon's brother, Sean. They hadn't returned in the period of time they'd hoped. That's why I've come to the World Above, why Shannon and I were in the forest. We're searching for our brothers."

"My father's fortress," Robin echoed. "But why? I would think that would be the last place a child of Duke Roland would wish to go, unless—"

"No," I said at once, cutting him off. "They did not go to cause your father harm. Jack was after the harp, the lyre."

"But that is madness!" Robin exclaimed. "Impossible. It's the only thing in all the world my father truly loves. He'd destroy anyone who tried to take it from him."

At his words, Shannon cried out. She buried her face in her hands. Only a supreme act of will kept me from doing the same. *Heaven help me, what will I tell Mama?* I wondered.

"You think they are dead, then," I said.

"I think," Robin said, and I had the feeling he was choosing his words with great care, "that we should make no assumptions. Acting on what you fear instead of what you know is never a wise choice. Let us wait for morning. It may be that one of the other scouts has more information."

Robin got to his feet. "I will say good night now."

Shannon and I rose also. My body felt as if it was made of lead, but within my chest, my heart burned with a fierce and painful fire. However, though he was now standing, Robin made no move to go.

"I hope your worst fears have not been realized," he said in a tense voice. "If it lies within my power, I will save your brothers. In the meantime, I will protect you as I protect my own people. You have shown them kindness, and I am grateful for it."

"Thank you," Shannon said softly.

Robin turned to go. He took a few steps, then stopped short. I could not see his face. All I could see was a dark outline.

"Gen des Jardins," he said quietly.

"I am listening," I replied.

"I hope your future in the World Above is brighter than you now have reason to believe it will be."

With that, he was gone.

SIXTEEN

We broke camp the following morning. In the daylight, I realized that Robin's encampment was much larger than I had previously supposed. Yet it was being dismantled with efficiency. Everyone seemed to have an assigned task, even the youngest ones.

Together Shannon and I figured out how to disassemble the tent. One of the women brought us each a rucksack. I folded the blankets and placed them inside. To this I added the remaining food from our saddlebags. I filled the waterskins at the river and added them, too.

Well, I guess we're as ready as we'll ever be.

Though I heard murmured discussion all around me, not once did I overhear grumbling about the need for our sudden departure. Aside from the woman who'd provided the rucksacks, no one approached us. Robin's people performed their tasks in determined silence, speaking only as was necessary to get the job done.

Finally everyone was ready. Robin assembled us all by the riverside. He stood with his back to the rushing water. Steel was beside him. Shannon and I stood together a short distance from the others. Trip suddenly appeared at my side. With him was a woman I judged to be about ten years older than I was. She carried a young child, who was sleeping peacefully in her arms. Our eyes met, and she smiled.

"You are Mad Tom's wife," I guessed aloud. The young woman nodded, her expression pleased. "What are you called?"

"Brave Hannah," she replied.

I laughed. From the corner of my eye, I saw Robin's head turn toward the sound.

"Is your child feeling better?"

"He is," Brave Hannah said. She gazed down at the little one in her arms, the love clear in her eyes. "He ate that bread and broth. I told young Trip I wished to thank you in person. I hear you gave all of your bread to strangers. There aren't many who'd have done a thing like that."

"Only every person here, or so I should imagine," I replied. "You were all strangers once, weren't you? But you aren't anymore."

"So you understand the way things work," she said.

"I do," I said. "At least I think so."

"I'll wish you good luck, then," Brave Hannah said.

"And to you," I answered. "Do you know where you will go?"

"That's up to Robin," Brave Hannah said. "Look, he's about to speak. I'd best be getting back to my husband now."

With another quick smile, she disappeared into the crowd. Trip stayed behind. Robin took a step forward, and just like that, the murmured conversations quieted.

"My friends," Robin said in a clear voice. "Thank you for making such quick work of your homes. We've had a lot of practice, haven't we?"

"That's true," I heard the people around me say. "What Robin says is true enough."

"I had hoped those days were coming to an end," Robin continued. "But it appears I got ahead of myself. By now you know why we must break camp. Our scouts have sighted my father's soldiers as far as the Boundary Oak. There's no reason to believe that they'll stop there. For safety, we must now split up."

"Why would they come so far, Robin?" a man's voice asked. "Why now, when they never have before?"

"I cannot say for certain," Robin answered. For a fraction of a second, his eyes met mine. "But it may be a cause for us to hope. The dream so many of us have cherished for so long has come true. Duke Roland's family survived. His heirs have returned."

Exclamations of astonishment spread through the crowd like lightning. I was feeling amazed myself. If I was truly understanding Robin's words, my mother hadn't been the only one telling stories. Someone had been spreading tales about Duke Roland's heirs.

Rowan, the old wise woman, I thought.

"All of you know the way I feel," Robin went on as he raised a hand for silence. "I have no quarrel with Duke Roland's heirs. Nothing would give me greater joy than to see his lands in the hands of the rightful rulers once more.

"My father is a usurper. His rule is unjust, not merely when it comes to Duke Roland's subjects, but his own as well. All of you assembled here know this. You have all felt the pain of what my father calls justice."

A murmur of assent passed through the crowd.

"But it may be that Duke Roland's son is now my father's prisoner," Robin said. "Or he may have already forfeited his life. The only way to know for sure is for me to return to my father's lands to discover the truth myself. I ask for a small group of volunteers to accompany me. No more than twenty or so. The rest of you, I ask to disperse among our other camps in the forest.

"Be vigilant. Exercise care. Stay out of sight. When I know what must be done, I will send word to all of you about the parts that you can play. Brave Hannah has agreed to take charge of the women with children."

"For shame, Robin," a woman's voice suddenly called out. "Are we not strong fighters?"

"You are, indeed," Robin answered, his face lighting in an unexpected smile. "But not good listeners, it seems. I said women *with* children, not women *and* children."

From the quick laughter, I knew that this was an old argument.

"It is good for us to laugh together," Robin said. "It makes me glad to hear it, but make no mistake, those of you who choose to accompany me will be going into great danger. No one should come who does not clearly understand the risk. There is no shame in staying behind."

"Robin speaks the truth, as always," Steel said. "We will need smart and able folk to stay behind— those you would trust to lead you should the worst befall us."

"But you'll succeed," a young man declared. "You'll never fail. You'll win and come back to us, Robin."

"I thank you for the faith you have in me," Robin said. "I'll do my best to deserve it. Now, quickly, all of you. I know many of you have already decided the paths you will take. Slowpoke and the other scouts have already agreed to follow me. Anyone else wishing to volunteer, come speak with Steel now."

Steel stepped aside, and a knot of men surrounded him. Robin moved through the crowd, bending low to speak to a child here and there, clasping hands of men and women both, gazing steadily into their eyes.

So young, I thought. Not much older than Jack and me, and yet it was clear that Robin was a leader, one whose people loved him. *He will make a fine duke one day*, I thought, and wondered if we would ever see that day come.

"He is very good at this, isn't he?" Shannon observed quietly.

"Funny you should say that," I answered. "I was just thinking the same thing. I wonder if Duke Guy knows his son is no longer a boy. He is a force to be reckoned with, he and his followers."

"The two of you would make a fine pair," she remarked.

My heart gave a sudden jolt.

"*What?*"

"Well, it only makes good sense, doesn't it?" she went on in a deceptively neutral voice. "Duke Guy's son and Duke Roland's daughter. You with your common sense and Robin with his charisma. It would make an elegant, yet simple, solution to a potential problem."

"You speak of practical considerations, then," I said, and wondered why my heart refused to beat as normal. Instead it was racing as if on an adventure of its own. Shannon's words had simply opened the door.

"Well, of course I do," Shannon replied, the slightest hint of mischief in her voice. "Did you think I was speaking of more?"

"I think," I said succinctly, "that I will box your ears if you keep this up."

"Just planting a seed," she said lightly. "I'm good at that, you know. Oh, look. Here comes Steel. I think they must be done deciding."

"Robin proposes that the two of you come with us," Steel said as he approached.

"He wants to take us into danger, then?" I asked.

"No," Steel said with a swift shake of his head. "Just the opposite. But he did not think either of you would agree to stay behind."

"He's right about that," Shannon said.

"It's settled then," Steel said. "We're ready."

Robin's people dispersed. Some families stayed together, others split up. But though I saw some sorrow and trepidation, I saw not an ounce of discontent.

They do more than simply follow Robin, I realized. *They make choices for themselves.* Robin let his people choose their own fates, as much as the circumstances would allow.

Definitely a force to be reckoned with, I thought, and recalled that I was pretty good at planting seeds myself. What might grow between Robin de Trabant and myself? Only time would show.

SEVENTEEN

We walked at a brisk pace set by Robin and Steel. As had been the case during our first journey with them, Robin and his band moved purposefully yet quietly. Again, we did not move as a single group but in an ever-changing sequence of pairs, each following the other. Slowpoke and several of the other scouts ranged ahead on their own. Shannon quickly settled into step alongside Steel.

I walked at Robin's side.

Whether this was by happenstance or choice on his part, I could not quite decide. For the first few hours, he didn't speak at all, completely lost in thought. But he was not so lost to his surroundings that he failed to offer assistance: holding aside a branch for me to pass, touching my elbow to guide me around a patch of damp earth so that we'd leave behind no footsteps.

For my part, I did my best not to distract Robin

from his thoughts. I figured he was entitled to them. I had a few things to think about myself.

Shortly before midday we came to a place where we would have to cross the river once more. The water moved quickly over a bed of stones. Several large, flat rocks protruded above the surface. They looked like stepping-stones.

"That's how we cross, isn't it?" I asked, pointing. Without thinking, I laid my other hand on Robin's arm. He started, and I backed up a step, hands in the air now to show I meant no harm. "I'm sorry," I said. "I—"

"No, don't," Robin said quickly. "It's nothing. I was lost in my thoughts. You surprised me, that's all."

He smiled suddenly, the expression lighting up his whole face. "I mean that as a compliment. You move well, quickly and silently as my own folk have learned to do. I forgot you haven't been one of us for very long. But to answer your question, yes, that is how we cross. You'll want to go carefully. The stones will be slick. I've taken an unintended dunking more than once."

He might as well have told me we were going to flap our arms and fly across the river for all the attention I paid to his advice. I was still stuck fast on the fact that he'd referred to me as "one of us."

It's just a figure of speech. Get ahold of yourself, Gen, I thought.

"I'll go first," Robin proposed, "since I've done this before."

"Just so long as you don't fall backward and drag me down with you," I replied.

"I'll remember you said that when you fall sideways and I have to pull you out," he came right back.

We grinned at each other. *It's so easy to tease him,* I thought. *Easier than I thought it might be. Might it be just as easy to fall in love?*

One moment. That's all it would take. A moment to let my guard down. A moment for my heart to make a leap into the unknown.

"I'm ready when you are," I said, then wondered which I was speaking to, my conversation with Robin or my own inner monologue.

In the end, no one fell backward or sideways. Instead I fell forward and almost drenched us both.

It happened as we were almost across the river. Robin had one foot on the bank and one on the very last stone. I had literally been following in his footsteps, of course, and I had done well. But I had to hold my skirts up with one hand, and this made keeping my balance on the slippery stones more of a challenge.

As I had throughout my passage, I tested my footing before I transferred all my weight forward. I had just done so on the next to last stone when, in spite of my best efforts, I could feel my foot begin to slide out from under me. I gave a cry. Releasing my skirts, I cartwheeled my arms in the air in an attempt to keep my balance.

"Gen!" Robin called out.

In the next moment, one of his hands wrapped

around my wrist. With a yank that snapped my head back, he pulled me forward, pivoting as he did so. His arm wrapped itself around my waist, and then suddenly it felt like we were flying. We landed on the hard earth of the river bank with enough force to knock the air from my lungs. I lay for a moment, trying to catch my breath, gazing up at the tops of the trees and the impossible blue of the sky.

"At least we didn't get wet," I said, when I had my breath back.

Robin began to laugh. To this day, I don't think I've ever heard so joyful a sound.

"Gen des Jardins," he finally said, "you are full of surprises."

"I'm really not," I protested. "I'm the practical one. Just ask Jack or Mama. They'll tell you."

All of a sudden my desire to laugh vanished. Jack was in danger. He might even be dead. How could I have forgotten, even for a moment? I felt a rush of tears fill my eyes. Embarrassed, I turned my head away. With gentle fingers, Robin reached to turn my head back, leveraging himself up on one elbow so that he could look down into my face.

"When we find out about your brother, whatever the news, I am going to find a way to make it right, Gen. I am not my father."

"I know you're not," I whispered. "But if Jack is gone . . ."

"If Jack is gone, then I can never bring him back," Robin said, his gaze steady on mine. "Just as I can never undo what my father did to yours. But I will do my best to change the future, to make certain such things never happen again. I want all our people to be free, and your rights to be restored. Do you believe me?"

"I believe you," I said, and with the words, I discovered that I had lost the desire to cry. "I want the same thing, and one thing more."

"What is that?" Robin asked.

"I want you to be happy in this future," I said. "I don't think you've known much happiness in the past."

Robin's face changed, pain and wonder combined. "I will do my best," he said again. "But, Gen—"

"Gen!" I heard Shannon cry out sharply. "Robin, what's wrong?"

Robin rolled away at once. He scrambled to his feet, then reached down a hand to pull me up beside him. Now that I was on my feet once more, I could see Shannon and Steel hastening toward us.

"There's nothing wrong," Robin replied. "Gen just had a little difficulty getting across the stream, that's all."

"Don't tell me," Steel said as they approached. His words were light, but I saw the way his eyes darted quickly between us, as if to assess Robin's claim that all was well. "It was that next to last stone, wasn't it?"

"So it's a known trickster," I said, determined to keep my tone light. "I think you might have warned me, Robin."

"I am dutifully chastened," he said, though he

didn't sound sorry at all. "Am I the only one who's hungry? As long as we are met, let us have our midday meal."

By design or happenstance, I wasn't sure which, Shannon and I switched companions following our meal. She accompanied Robin, while I walked with Steel. Part of me was relieved; the other part was disappointed.

Both are unlike you, Gen, I thought. I definitely seemed more prone to extremes since coming to the World Above.

"Thank you for agreeing to walk with me," Steel said, his tone somewhat formal. "I wasn't sure that you would want to."

I came to a full stop. "Steel," I said. "Can we please get something straight right here and now? I don't dislike you."

"But you don't quite like me either," he responded.

"I don't *know* you," I replied. "You don't know me."

"True enough," Steel said. We continued on in silence. Robin and Shannon were no longer in sight.

Oh, nicely done, Gen, I thought as we walked along. *Offend the man who thinks he's just as responsible for your father's death as Guy de Trabant himself.*

"Are there really tales that claim Duke Roland's heir would someday return?" I asked after a moment.

"There are," Steel answered promptly. "They began not long after your father's death. No one knows quite how they started."

"Oh, but surely Rowan, the wise woman . . . ," I began, then stopped. There was something about the set of Steel's shoulders, the determined lack of expression on his face. "It was you, wasn't it?"

Steel did not reply.

"But why?" I asked, certain that I was right. "Duke Roland was dead. What could you possibly hope to accomplish?"

"To be a thorn in Guy de Trabant's side, if nothing else," Steel admitted quietly. "But also . . . to make amends, though I know that is impossible. To tell you the truth, I never expected the stories I spread to reach so many. But the people truly loved your parents. They were eager to hope that your mother might have survived, that she might have secretly given birth to Duke Roland's heir. She disappeared so quickly and was so well hidden. It was not as far-fetched as it sounds."

"Will you tell me something else?" I asked. "Will you tell me what happened the night my father died?"

"Are you sure you really want to hear it?" Steel asked.

"No, I'm not," I replied honestly. "But I've had to do a lot of things I didn't initially want to do. Maybe this should be one of them. And I think perhaps it would be good for both of us if you were to tell me."

"There isn't all that much to tell," Steel began. "My father was Duke Roland's seneschal. He helped to run his estates and to organize all his public functions."

"A well-educated man," I said, then decided to hazard a guess. "But not a soldier."

"No." Steel shook his head. "He was trained in weapons as every man of his station was, of course, but his purpose in the castle was not to be a man-at-arms."

And neither was yours, I thought.

"How did you come to be with my father that night?" I asked.

"Through Duke Roland's kindness," Steel answered at once. "I was quick with my lessons, even as a boy. Duke Roland collected manuscripts."

"I didn't know that," I said.

"Did you not?" Steel asked, surprised. "I thought perhaps your mother might have told you."

"To tell you the truth," I said slowly, thinking back, "she really doesn't talk about him very much. Not in the way you and I are talking now. Until lately, everything Jack or I ever knew about the World Above we learned from my mother's bedtime stories. Mostly she told about how she'd made her escape, how we all ended up living in the World Below."

"Your mother was very brave, to go so far all on her own," Steel said.

"Yes," I said. "I suppose she was, but you're trying to change the subject."

Steel boosted himself up onto an enormous tree trunk that had fallen across our way. He reached down to take my hand, then pulled me up beside him. Hands still clasped, we jumped down on the far side, the floor of the Greenwood, soft with fallen leaves, cushioning our landing.

"It was just a particular set of circumstances that put me in Duke Roland's rooms that night," he went on. He released his hold on my hand. "Your mother was away, the duke had a new manuscript, and I was visiting my father. I had recently returned after visiting my mother's people."

"How old were you?" I asked.

"Eighteen," Steel answered shortly. "When Duke Roland learned that I was in the castle, he sent for me. He wanted to show me the new manuscript. I remember it was a quiet autumn evening, just cool enough for a fire. Duke Roland sent his retainers away. I've often thought . . . if he'd been better guarded . . ."

"It might not have made a difference," I said quietly. "He didn't think to guard for a danger from within."

"No," Steel said, his tone grim. "He did not. We had just begun to pore over the manuscript when the door burst open. They were on us almost before I could reach for my sword."

"Was Guy de Trabant with them?" I asked.

Steel shook his head. "No. But we could hear his voice, shouting. I remember having time to think, 'It will be all right. Lord Guy is coming. He will stop them.' Then he came through the door. There was something about the look on his face." Steel shook his head, as if to shake out the ugly memory. "There was such a strange, wild light in his eyes."

"You knew," I said.

"I knew," Steel echoed. "And so did Duke Roland. Guy de Trabant had not come to save us. I began to struggle. I remember Duke Roland's voice saying, 'Guy, not the boy.' Then something hit me in the head. I saw blood, but I couldn't tell whose it was, mine or Duke Roland's. By the time I knew myself again, it was over. Your father was dead, and Guy de Trabant had seized the castle."

"It's a miracle he let you live," I said.

"It is." Steel nodded. "I've never understood why."

"Perhaps he simply decided there'd been enough killing," I said. "My father's death was the only one he really needed, after all."

"Duke Roland saved me," Steel said, his voice filled with emotion. "I couldn't save him. All my life, I've been sorry for it."

We continued in silence. It was painful to hear about my father's death, the untimely end of a good man, a man who had been loved. But not so painful that I couldn't bear it. I had never had the chance to know him, after all. But Steel had carried the burden of that night for many years.

"I'm glad my father had someone he loved with him at the end," I finally said. "Perhaps that is also a way to think about what happened that night. Guy de Trabant's betrayal must have hurt my father deeply. He had loved him like a son. But Duke Roland died knowing your life would be spared, and because of you, he did not die alone."

"You are very generous," Steel said, after a moment.

"No," I said. "I'm not. I'm just practical. And you've given me a gift, even if it is a painful one. You have brought my father to life, if only for a moment. You've shown me how generous *he* was."

"I'm sure Duke Roland would be proud to know you were his daughter," Steel said.

Now it was my turn to become grim. "Even though I failed to save his son?"

"You don't know that," Steel said swiftly. "None of us does."

"You're right," I said, with a lift of my chin. "We don't."

What was it Shannon had said as we stood before my parents' portrait? Jack wasn't the only one who resembled my father. I did too, in my determination. It was time to demonstrate it now, time to prove I was Duke Roland's child. *His true heir*, I thought. For that is precisely what I was.

"Are we friends now?" I asked.

"Yes," Steel said. "I believe that we are."

"In that case, I wonder if I might ask you to tell me one last thing."

"What's that?" he asked, though I thought I could tell from the smile on his face that he knew perfectly well.

"What's your real name?" I asked.

"Gerard."

"Gerard," I said, rolling the sound of it around in my mouth. "It's nice, but I think that I like Steel better. It suits you, somehow."

"I have grown accustomed to it," Steel answered. "But it is good to remember the lad that I once was. You have given me that gift."

"So we are friends and we are even," I said. "What could be better than that?"

"Hush!" Steel said suddenly. He stopped walking abruptly, holding up a hand for silence. His head whipped from side to side. "Fool, idiot," I heard him swear. "So lost in the past you forgot to pay attention to the present."

"What is it?" I whispered urgently. "What?"

Before he could even draw breath to answer, we were surrounded by Duke Guy's soldiers.

EIGHTEEN

Instantly Steel moved to shield me, thrusting me behind him. *That will make no difference,* I thought. The soldiers encircled us. I spun so that Steel and I stood back-to-back. *Futile!* I thought. All I had done was to make it possible to look my attackers in the face. I had no weapon to fight with. No way to defend myself.

"Well, lads, what have we here?" a rough voice spoke.

That must be the leader, I thought. He had a face that looked as if it had taken a few blows. His nose dominated his face. I wondered how many times it had been broken.

The band of soldiers was small, no more than half a dozen. But that would be more than enough to capture a man with only a knife, and a girl with only her wits and courage to defend herself.

Wits. Use your wits, Gen, I thought. Robin and the

others could not be that far off. Perhaps, if I could keep the soldiers talking, get them to make enough noise . . .

"What on earth do you think you have?" I snapped. "Are you stupid, or can't you see beyond the end of that great nose of yours? Haven't you ever seen a father and daughter out foraging for mushrooms? You've no right to stop us. We've done nothing wrong."

"You're a spitfire, that's for sure," the captain spoke once more. He tossed the short sword he carried from hand to hand, as if deciding which to use when he cut us to pieces. "What's the matter with your father? Cat got his tongue?"

At that, the woods around us erupted in a great roar. A man dashed out from the stand of trees just behind the captain. He seemed as tall as one of the trees he'd sheltered behind. In one hand he carried a branch, which he brought crashing down over the captain's head before he could so much as turn around.

Mayhem broke out. Half the soldiers rushed to take on the attacker, while the other half turned tail and ran for their lives. Steel leaped forward to help press the attack. Almost before I could catch my breath, it was all over. Steel and the newcomer stood facing each other. Four of Duke Guy's soldiers lay on the ground.

"I don't know who you are, but we are grateful for your help," Steel began, though he had to tip his head back to look into our rescuer's eyes. "Without you . . ."

The giant's eyes had moved from Steel's face to find mine.

"Gen," he said. "I'd know you anywhere."

"And you can only be Sean."

Before I could say another word, Robin rushed into the clearing, with Shannon following close behind. Slowpoke and a group of scouts approached from the opposite side.

"It's all right," Slowpoke said. "We got them, Robin."

"*Sean!*" Shannon cried out. She ran toward him.

Sean caught Shannon in an embrace, lifting her off her feet to hold her close. I could see his lips move as he whispered something in her ear. Shannon shook her head fiercely and buried her face in his throat. In spite of the difference in their statures, brother and sister looked a great deal alike. Sean had Shannon's curly hair, though his was cropped close.

"Shan," he said, his voice a deep rumble in his chest. "Come on, now. Don't act like such a girl."

One of Shannon's dangling feet shot out to kick him in the leg.

"There now," Sean said. "That's the Shannon I know and love."

"Giant," she accused as he set her on her feet.

"Pip-squeak," he responded. Her head barely reached above Sean's waist, and her arms couldn't quite reach all the way around it.

"Where's Jack? What's happened to him? Why aren't you together?" she demanded.

"If you'll stop talking, I'll tell you," Sean said. "Jack is alive. He's also Duke Guy's prisoner."

"Getting to the town was easy enough," Sean explained a short time later. Several of the scouts had gone back out to search for any additional soldiers. Satisfied that we were safe for the time being, Robin had called a halt so we could hear Sean's story.

"It took Jack and me about a week to reach Duke Guy's fortress, just like we'd thought it would," Sean explained. "Once we got there, we agreed to split up. It seemed safest that way." He made a face. "I tend to draw attention to myself. But we arranged a place to meet each night.

"During the days, Jack did his best to familiarize himself with the layout of the town. I plotted possible escape routes through the forest. Both of us waited for the assizes."

Robin's face had worn a frown of concentration through Sean's recital. But at the mention of the court of appeals, Robin's face cleared and he began to nod.

Quick. He is so quick, I thought.

"You thought to use the assizes to get close to the harp," he said. "My father always makes use of it there, and it's one of the few times he actually lets it out of arm's reach, though hardly out of sight."

Abruptly Robin got to his feet and began to pace, as if trying to work out the way things must have gone.

"But you couldn't just snatch it, could you? It's too heavily guarded."

"That's right," Sean acknowledged. "But Jack wasn't ready to give up. We knew we had four weeks before you'd come after us, Gen."

"So you decided to wait for a second session," I said.

Sean nodded. "This time I was to accompany Jack. He'd told me how the assizes worked overall—where the harp was placed, how many men guarded it, how it was transported. But he wanted a second pair of eyes, just to make sure he hadn't missed anything."

Sean gave me a crooked smile. "He was trying to think like you, Jack said. He was trying to build a plan. But for all that, it was hopeless. The session was almost over for the day when a fight broke out. It happened so quickly I never did know what it was about."

"Don't tell me," I said, as what must have happened next came clear in a flash. "Jack improvised."

"He did." Sean nodded. "But it was really all my fault, because I'm so tall. I could see what no one else could, not even Duke Guy himself. For a few precious moments, the harp was left unguarded.

"The fight was sudden and fierce. One moment everything was calm. In the next, it was pandemonium. Half of Guy de Trabant's soldiers waded into the fray. The other half rushed to protect the duke himself. In the confusion, the soldiers forgot all about guarding the harp."

"So you took it," Shannon breathed. "*You* took it, not Jack. Oh, Sean."

"I knew how much it meant to him," Sean said, his tone pleading. "I used the confusion to get to Jack and give him the harp. He was more likely to be able to slip away, because he's—you know—the same size as most people, and the harp really did belong to him, after all. But the harp . . . the harp . . ."

His voice choked with emotion.

"The harp began to sing, didn't it?" Robin asked quietly. He stopped pacing and reached out to lay a hand on the giant's shoulder. Seated, Sean's shoulder was almost the same height as Robin's.

"The harp began to sing," echoed Sean. "I'd heard the sound it made as it helped Duke Guy pass judgment. But this was something different, something more. Never in my life have I heard such a sound. I don't think . . ." He twisted his head to look into Robin's face. "I'm not sure I have the words to describe it."

"I think I may," Robin said quietly. From across the clearing, he met my eyes. "It sang for me, the one and only time I touched it. I'm still not sure I understand why.

"Imagine the sound that you love best, the one that never fails to fill your heart with joy. Perhaps it's a sound you remember from childhood. Or maybe it's a sound that's been silenced forever, your mother's voice singing a lullaby. Whatever that sound is, the voice of the harp is as beautiful, and more. Once you have heard it, you will never forget."

"I could never have described it like that," Sean said. "But that's how it was. The second I put the harp into Jack's hands, it began to sing. At first it was just a note—a tone. But then it began to call out a single word: 'Master! Master!'"

"The harp called out for Guy de Trabant?" I exclaimed, astonished.

"No," Sean said. "Though I thought so at first myself. But I've had a lot of time to think about it since. I think your plan worked, Gen. Reclaiming the wizard's gifts was the best way to demonstrate your birthright. Somehow that harp recognized Jack. It knew who he was."

"His true master," Robin said. "Roland des Jardins' son."

"But the harp gave him away," Sean said in a tortured voice. "The moment it began to sing, the soldiers surrounded Jack. It was terrible. For a moment I thought . . ."

"You thought they would kill him," I said.

Sean nodded. "But they did not. They dragged him forward, the harp still in his hands, and threw him at Guy de Trabant's feet. The expression on de Trabant's face when he got a good look at Jack almost stopped my heart."

"He recognized him too," I said. "He must have, Jack looks so much like our father. Anyone who had seen Duke Roland would know Jack was his son."

"What happened then?" Shannon asked, anguish in her voice.

"The soldiers took Jack away," Sean said. "They dispersed the crowd. And then . . . nothing. For days the town was locked up tight. It was impossible to get close to the fortress. Then, about two days ago, Guy de Trabant sent out his heralds."

"That would be when the soldiers appeared at the Boundary Oak," Robin murmured.

"There's to be an execution," I said. It felt as though a band of iron was wrapped around my heart.

"No," Sean said quickly. "Something more complicated, more cunning." He turned to Robin. "You know the harvest festival is just a few days off?"

"Of course," Robin said, nodding.

"There's to be an addition to the festivities," Sean explained. "An archery contest. Duke Guy has a champion archer who will compete against all comers. If he is unbeaten, the duke's cause will be deemed just and the prisoner will be executed the following morning."

Shannon gave a low moan. She doubled over, as if all the strength she usually displayed was folding in on itself.

"And if the champion is defeated?" I asked, though I felt like I was suffocating.

"Then the winner will have earned the right to decide the prisoner's fate," said Sean. "Duke Guy agrees to be bound by the outcome."

"So all we have to do is to find someone who can outshoot the champion," I said, buoyed by a surge of unexpected hope. "Just how good is he? Can it be done?"

"Oh, it can be done," Robin answered. "It *has* been done, but only once."

"Well then, that settles things!" Shannon cried. She shot to her feet, all her earlier energy restored. "We find the man who bested him and get him to do it again." At the look on Sean's face, she broke off. "What?"

"I don't know this for sure," Sean said, his tone apologetic. "It's just what I heard them say in the town. It's why I thought I must come to the forest myself, to try and find Guy de Trabant's son."

"It's you, isn't it?" I asked. "You're the one who can defeat the archer."

"The only one," Robin admitted. "A fact my father knows quite well. In fact, it's what he's counting on. His trap is just like he is, cunning and subtle. If I don't show up, not only will I brand myself a coward, I'll have an innocent man's death on my conscience."

"But if you do appear, and best the champion for a second time . . ."

"Then my father wins on all counts," Robin completed my thought. "He will have both me and Duke Roland's son within his power. He can do whatever he wants with both of us."

NINETEEN

Robin immediately began to make preparations for Jack's rescue. The archery contest was set for the following day. That didn't give us much time. Robin sent Slowpoke and the quickest of the other scouts back through the forest to find the others and notify them of what was going on. As many of Robin's people as could be assembled were to come to the archery field to mingle among the crowds.

Steel, who was not known in Duke Guy's lands, volunteered to go on ahead to reconnoiter the town. That left Robin, Sean, Shannon, and me to proceed together, along with the few remaining scouts. In less time than I might have dreamed possible, our small band had dispersed. Steel would be the last to depart.

Robin was going to try to save Jack, no matter what.

"Will you walk with me a moment, Gen?" Robin

asked. "There is something I would like to show you."

"Go ahead, Gen," Shannon said quickly. "Sean and I will go with the scouts."

Robin set a brisk pace, brisk enough to make conversation impractical, though not quite impossible. As we walked, long shadows began to fall. *It will be dark soon,* I thought. *All our fates will be decided tomorrow.*

I tried to think of a way to help. Some fallback plan I could provide. Making plans was supposed to be what I was best at, but I couldn't seem to get my mind to focus. It skittered back and forth like a mouse in a trap.

If Robin did nothing, I would lose Jack for sure. But if he participated in the archery contest and could not escape his father's trap in time, I would lose them both.

Think, Gen. Think! I told myself. *Don't just use your head. Use your heart.*

"Where are we going?" I asked.

"To the Boundary Oak. It's not far. I thought you might like to see it, and I find . . ." Robin frowned. "I find I've suddenly discovered a superstitious streak in my nature. The Boundary Oak is a testament to the way things ought to be. I would like to see it again myself."

One last time, I thought, hearing in my head the words he did not speak aloud. *But it won't be. I won't let it.*

"Gen," Robin suddenly said. He stopped and

turned me toward him with his hand on my arm. "If things go wrong tomorrow—"

"No," I said fiercely. I reached up to cover his hand with mine. We were standing face-to-face. One more step and we would have been in each other's arms.

"I don't want to hear it, Robin. Call it my own superstitious nature, if you will. I don't want to talk about what will happen if we fail. I want to think of a way for us to beat the odds."

"They're stacked pretty high against us," he said.

"What difference does that make?" I answered stubbornly. "We just have to try harder. I keep thinking there must be a way out, or at least around."

"I hope you're right," Robin said.

"You listen to me, Robin de Trabant," I said. "I am not going to lose you now. Not you and not Jack, not both at once."

"You would be sorry, then, if I never came back?" Robin asked softly.

"Don't be an idiot," I said, and suddenly we were both smiling.

"Gen des Jardins," he murmured. "Always full of surprises."

"Show me this tree," I said. "Perhaps it will inspire me."

"It's not much farther now," Robin said. He continued walking. But he kept my hand in his, our fingers linked tightly. "There," he said, a few moments later.

We stood at the base of a small rise. At the summit was a clearing, still bright with fading sunlight.

Whether it had been created naturally, or by those who had planted the tree long ago, I did not know. In the clearing's center stood an enormous oak. The trunk was broad, its thick limbs outstretched. A scattering of acorns lay on the ground. As we made our approach, a breeze came up, causing thick clusters of brown leaves to tumble to the ground.

Something is not right here, I thought.

"Robin," I said, my voice little more than a whisper. "I fear this tree is dying."

Now that I knew what to look for, I could see that it was so. The great trunk was rent by a deep divide. Though autumn had begun to come on, the leaves should still be green. Instead they were dry and brittle, prematurely brown. Even I, who have never been fanciful, could almost feel the effort the oak was making simply to stay alive. It was a battle the tree was losing, day by day.

"This is my father's doing. I know it," Robin said in a ravaged voice. "It is the sickness his rule brings on the land. It is wrong; it is false, and even this tree knows it."

I let go of his hand and moved to place my palms against the great trunk. It seemed to me that I could feel the oak's heart, all the possibilities for the future, striving against the blight that Guy de Trabant brought to both the lands the tree had been planted to honor.

"This tree is like you," I said. "It has not given up."

"Then tell me how I can prevail!" Robin cried. "It

seems to me that my father holds all the cards. The only thing I've ever successfully accomplished is running away. I don't even truly fight him. All I do is deprive fat merchants of their wares."

"You've done something your father never has," I said. "You've won the people's love."

"And I am grateful for it," Robin replied, his voice more calm. "It's the only reason no one's ever claimed the bounty on my head."

"What does your father offer?" I asked, suddenly curious as to the price Guy de Trabant had set on the life of his only son.

"The most precious thing he has to offer," Robin answered bitterly. "Duke Roland's harp. In exchange for turning me in, my betrayer may use the lyre just as my father does."

"You mean they get to ask questions?" I said sharply. "And the harp will say whether the answers received are true or not?"

"Three questions," Robin said. "Just like three wishes."

"And they may be posed of anyone?"

"Anyone." Robin nodded, a faint frown between his brows. "And the person chosen will be compelled to answer. My father has sworn it."

The harp, I thought, and I felt my thoughts begin to tumble and whirl like the fall of leaves around me. *The lyre that could sing with its own voice and could never tell a lie.*

What if the wizard had bestowed a gift even

greater than he himself knew? What if he had provided the means to save us all?

"You have an idea," Robin said. "Tell me what it is."

I took my hands from the tree and pressed them against the sides of my head, as if to help organize my thoughts.

"Tell me something first," I said.

"Anything."

"Why did you run away from home?"

"What difference does that make?" Robin asked.

"Please," I said.

"All right," Robin said. "It isn't very honorable, I'm afraid. I left because I simply couldn't stand it anymore. I couldn't stand to see the man my father had become. I couldn't bear the thought that I might grow to be just like him."

"And what is that?"

"Broken," Robin answered shortly. "Bitter and frightened when he might have been honorable. But I think what I hated most were the times I caught glimpses of the man my father might have been, if not for what he'd done to Duke Roland."

Robin paused, as if struggling with his remembrances. His hands clenched at his sides.

"It's true what they say about me, you know," he continued. "I did run wild. But I was never wild for the pleasure of it and nothing more. I ran wild so that my father and I would both know that I was different, that I would never grow to be the kind of man that he was. The kind who would betray a trust.

"In the end, it made no difference at all. My father betrayed trust for me. He sent his soldiers into the city. He snatched families from their homes. That was the night I knew I had to leave for good. That was the night that I stopped loving him."

"I'm not so sure you did," I said. "If you had, he couldn't hurt you nearly so much. And if he'd stopped loving you, he wouldn't try so hard to get you back."

"It's not for love," Robin denied swiftly. "It's policy. I'm a pawn to be played and nothing more."

"Are you absolutely certain of that?" I asked. I went to him then and seized him by the shoulders. "Are you sure there's nothing more? Are you willing to stake your life on it?"

"Tell me what is in your mind," Robin said. "Tell me what your eyes see that mine do not."

I took a breath, and shared my thoughts.

But it was only after he had listened carefully and agreed to my proposal, only after we met up with Sean and Shannon and I had explained what must be done, only after the four of us were hastening toward our fates, that I realized I had left something out.

I had told Robin the secrets I thought his father's heart might hold, but I had failed to share the secrets of my own.

TWENTY

And so the final stage of my journey began. *I am on an adventure now in earnest,* I thought. For surely part of the definition of true adventure is the inability to see its outcome. I knew what I hoped, and I had convinced the others to believe in that hope with me. But whether or not our hopes would prevail and all would come out happily in the end . . . The answers to those questions would still have to wait.

Duke Guy's harvest festival looked much like those that Jack, Mama, and I had attended every year in the World Below. The houses in the town were decorated with cornstalks bound together with brightly colored ribbon, sheaves of grain, and vivid orange pumpkins.

The people were dressed in their holiday finery. But in spite of all this, with the exception of the very young children playing tag through the streets, the mood in the town did not seem joyful. Instead it seemed watchful.

Guy de Trabant's people have not been fooled, I thought. They knew that something dire was coming. I only hoped we could use this to our advantage. These people loved Robin. If need be, would they defy his father for him?

"We should head for the field," Shannon said in a low voice. "It's almost time for the archery contest."

In the two days since the announcement of the archery contest, Duke Guy's servants had been busy readying the field. A raised platform had been constructed halfway along one side. At its back, a series of banners snapped in the breeze. In its center stood Duke Guy's great chair. I wondered if it was the same one he had carried into the court of assizes.

Several other chairs sat alongside, though none was as grand as the duke's. On either side of the platform were sets of bleachers for Duke Guy's court. Beyond that was a place for the common people to stand, though many had already taken up places on the far side of the field, facing Duke Guy and his entourage.

And throughout, in every place where people gathered, Duke Guy's soldiers were also present. Shannon and I had seen the soldiers during the day, strolling through the streets as if they were on holiday. They weren't, though. Every man we saw had his breastplate freshly polished, his hand resting on the pommel of his sword. I wondered if any mingled with the crowds dressed as commoners. There was simply no way to tell.

In the center of the field stood a series of targets, side by side. Duke Guy's champion archer would shoot at one set, the challengers at the other.

"Look, there's Mad Tom," Shannon said, pointing to a familiar figure. He had secured a place at the very front of the crowd. As we'd strolled the streets of the town throughout the morning, Shannon and I had caught sight of others of Robin's people. We had acknowledged one another with a quick nod, but nothing more.

All Robin's people had been warned that something unusual might take place, and that they were not to interfere until Robin asked for their help himself. But of Robin or Steel themselves, Shannon and I had seen no sign. Robin's absence, I knew, was by design. After some discussion, we had decided it would be best to let Guy de Trabant wonder whether or not his son would take the bait. But concern over Steel's whereabouts was like the buzz of an angry bee in the back of my mind.

Had he been captured somehow? It hardly seemed likely. By his own admission, he was not known in Duke Guy's lands. No one could know that Steel belonged to Robin. We could have simply missed him in the crowd, of course. It was a large one. Still, the fact that we hadn't seen him at all bothered me.

A call of trumpets rang out.

Duke Guy must be arriving, I thought. Shannon and

I elbowed our way through the crowd, on our way to Mad Tom. All too soon now we would know whose strategy would succeed, Duke Guy's or mine.

The duke's bodyguards came first, marching smartly in his colors of green and gold. Then came several men I had no way to identify. *Chief nobles, or court functionaries,* I thought. The most elaborately dressed carried a bundle in his arms.

Surely that must be the harp, I thought.

The functionary moved to stand in front of a chair on the far side of Duke Guy's, though he did not sit down. The others of the duke's retinue now arranged themselves behind the row of chairs. There was a second fanfare of trumpets, and finally I saw Guy de Trabant himself.

He was tall, his bearing straight and proud, as if his very posture was a dare to all those who would defy him. He was dressed in fine garments of deep forest green. From his shoulders hung a bloodred cloak lined in cloth of gold.

But it was his face that caught my attention and held it. This man was not much older than my mother. Unlike her, he had led a rich and comfortable life. But above his fine clothes, Duke Guy's face bore the unmistakable marks of time. His hair was a shock of ashy gray. His eyes were sunk deep into their sockets. Grooves outlined the sides of his mouth. It seemed to me that this was the face of a man who knew no peace.

What might he do to find it? I wondered.

"Gen, look," Shannon's voice suddenly spoke at my side. Her grip on my arm was tight enough to cut off circulation.

Following Guy de Trabant, guarded by a second group of soldiers, walked a familiar form. I felt my heart begin to thunder in my chest. *Jack!* I thought. *Oh, please,* I prayed silently. *Let him not have been harmed.*

But as far as I could see, Jack seemed fine. He carried himself erect. His face was unmarked. In honor of the occasion, he'd been given a set of noble-man's clothes. But these could not disguise the fact that he was a prisoner. His hands were bound in front of him. The soldiers escorting him positioned themselves in a curve behind his chair and alongside it, as if to ensure that Jack could not dash down the steps at the end of the platform and make a run for it.

Duke Guy came to a halt in front of his chair of estate. As if from nowhere, a servant appeared to take the long cloak he wore. For a moment the duke stood, gazing out across the field, as if picturing what was to come in his mind. Then he sat, and everyone who had a place to do so sat down too.

The duke raised a hand, and a single trumpet called. As its notes died away, a man with a longbow and a quiver full of arrows strode onto the field, with a second man, dressed in Duke Guy's livery, at his side. *That is the herald,* I thought. Again the trumpet called. Though the crowd assembled on either side of the field was enormous, by the time the voice of the trumpet had faded, everyone had fallen silent.

They all know what is at stake today, I thought.

"I give you the duke's champion, Yves Dupré," the herald called out. "By Duke Guy's command, he will now accept all challengers. If any man can best the champion, he will win the right to determine the fate of the prisoner seated beside Duke Guy. But if the champion triumphs, the life of that same prisoner is forfeit to the crown."

The herald bowed toward Duke Guy. Then he marched smartly off the field, leaving the champion archer standing alone. He plucked an arrow from the quiver.

"I am ready," he declared.

The first challenger stepped up to face the target.

The archery contest continued well into the afternoon. The sun burned hot in the sky, but Duke Guy's champion showed no sign of growing tired. There were moments when it seemed to me that he possessed an almost superhuman strength. Man after man appeared to take up the challenge. The two men stood side by side, each facing a target. They took turns firing. If the arrows landed in more or less equal positions on the targets, the targets were moved back ten paces and the contestants repeated the ritual. But this didn't happen often. Yves Dupré defeated most of his challengers with a single shot.

Finally only three challengers remained. Second to last stood Robin. He was dressed like any other country man, in plain brown homespun. He wore a straw hat on his head, the brim shading his features. Still, there was nothing plain about him. There was simply no disguising Robin.

Do I only see this because I love him? I wondered suddenly. Or was it the plain and simple truth that there was nothing plain or simple about Robin? Always there would be something that set him apart, something more than an accident of noble birth.

It's all the things that aren't accidental, I thought. It was the way he had chosen to maintain a generous spirit and a sharp mind. Robin had something that his father did not. Much more important than noble bearing, Robin possessed a noble heart.

Yves Dupré dispatched the challenger ahead of Robin with two shots. And then, at long last, Robin was stepping up to the target. His movements were loose and easy, as if he were completely unaware of all the eyes upon him, completely unconcerned that two lives hung in the balance.

"Look," Mad Tom said in a low voice, as Robin removed his hat and dropped it to the ground. "Dupré knows him."

One look was all it took to see that this was so. Yves Dupré started, then made a movement as if to kneel. Robin stopped him with a hand on his arm. The two men spoke to each other. All around me, I could hear the voice of the crowd begin to swell, as more and more people began to speak of what they had seen. I looked at the platform. Guy de Trabant sat perfectly still, as if turned to stone.

Finally, the conversation between Robin and his father's champion archer seemed to end. Robin took his stance before the target, pulled an arrow from his quiver, and nocked it to his bow. The crowd hushed as he pulled back the string and let the arrow fly. It flew straight and true, the point burying itself in the center of the target. As if it had a single voice now, the crowd gave forth a moan.

They don't know what to think, I thought.

Now Yves Dupré took his turn. His arrow too found the perfect mark. At a signal from the herald, servants came forward and moved the targets back ten paces. Their order reversed, the two contenders shot a second time. Again both arrows found their marks. The targets were moved back ten more paces.

The crowd was growing restive now. *This is where their love for Robin will truly be put to the test,* I thought.

For Robin's people had spread the same instructions they had received themselves: No matter what happened, the crowd must not interfere, not until Robin gave the signal as a last resort. The plan I had devised must be given a chance to play itself out. But if the crowd's fear for Robin's safety led them to take action too soon . . .

It seemed to me as if the whole world held its breath as, for a third time, Robin sighted the target and let an arrow fly. Yet again it buried itself in the very center of the target. Duke Guy's champion put an arrow to his bow. The banners hung loosely on their poles, not a breath of wind to stir them as Yves

Dupré took his stance, pulling the string taut.

But then he seemed to hesitate. He continued to stand, legs spread, body as tight as his own bow string, and still he did not let the arrow go. Almost in spite of myself I began to count, *One, two, three*, in the silence of my mind.

That was when I heard it. The quick *snap* of the banners as the wind came up. As if the sound had been the signal for which he'd been waiting, Yves Dupré loosed his arrow. It streaked toward the target. The crowd gave a feral moan. Then, with a force that made the target rock, the arrow struck home.

Duke Guy surged to his feet. The herald sprinted for the target. *Close. It is so close*, I thought. But even as I saw Yves Dupré fall to his knees at last, even as I saw Robin place a hand on the other man's shoulder, I thought I understood what the champion archer had done. Instead of waiting for the wind to die down, he had waited for it to rise. The sudden burst of air had drawn his arrow off course.

Just a little. Just enough.

"The challenger is the winner!" the herald cried.

"*Now*, Gen," said Mad Tom.

I picked up my skirts and ran for all I was worth toward Robin, praying that the nerve of the crowd would hold.

"Bounty!" I shouted as I ran. "That man is Robert de Trabant. I claim the bounty on his head, according to Duke Guy's law!"

TWENTY-ONE

To this day, I'm not quite sure I know all of what happened next. My whole world became a sea of conflicting sights and sounds. I could see Yves Dupré, weeping at Robin's feet. All around me, I heard shouts from the crowd, and the duke's captain shouting orders to his soldiers. And finally I could hear Robin himself, calling out for the crowd to be still. To trust him and hold true to his cause if ever they had loved him.

Unbelievably, miraculously, it worked. Though the crowd moaned like an animal in pain, no one rushed forward to challenge the soldiers as they surrounded us. I stood beside Robin, gazing up into his face, battling the urge to weep.

This is the true magic of the World Above, I thought. *This demonstration that love truly can conquer fear.*

Now there was just one more person who must prove his love. The most unlikely one of all. I had staked everything on this one leap of faith: my belief that, despite all evidence to the contrary, despite what Robin himself believed, Duke Guy de Trabant loved his son.

Quickly now, the soldiers marched us toward the platform where Duke Guy stood, his courtiers and nobles clustered around him. Jack still stood to the side, surrounded by his guards. For several moments no one spoke. Robin stood still, gazing up at his father. Duke Guy looked back down. Even in the midst of turmoil, I felt my heart give a surge of hope. Duke Guy had eyes for no one but his son.

"You are looking tired, Father," Robin said at last.

A wintry smile touched Duke Guy's features. "And whose fault is that, my son? Let's get the first part of this over quickly, shall we?" He gestured toward Jack. "I suppose you intend to spare this young man's life?"

"Of course I do," Robin answered steadily. "Why else would I have come?"

"Why else, indeed?" his father inquired. "And I would grant your request, were it not for the fact that you are a criminal yourself. Can one wanted man free another? I'm not certain the law will allow that. It seems you have risked yourself for nothing, my son."

"Then do what the law *will* allow," I finally spoke up. "I named this man your son, when no one else would. I claim the bounty as my reward."

Duke Guy's eyebrows shot up. "Betrayed by a woman? That doesn't sound like you, Robert. Well, young woman, I will—"

"What you will do," a voice I recognized broke in, "is let all three of them go."

A lone figure stepped out from the body of the crowd. He, too, carried a bow, string pulled taut, the arrow nocked and ready to be let go. It pointed straight at Guy de Trabant.

"Steel," I moaned. "No."

"Do not speak to me," Steel said harshly. "You I will deal with in good time." He took a few steps closer. "Well, my lord?"

"Don't be a fool," Guy de Trabant snarled. He gestured to the soldiers, their weapons at the ready. "You will be dead yourself as soon as the arrow leaves the bow."

"As long as I take you with me, that will be enough," Steel replied. "Now give the order to release them, or I will release my arrow."

"Steel," Robin said in a low, clear voice.

"No!" Steel said. "Do not try and stop me, Robin."

"Do you love me?" Robin asked, as if his friend had not spoken. "Do you trust my judgment?"

"You know I do," Steel said. "More than my own life."

"Then listen to me," Robin said. "Do not fire."

"Think what you are asking!"

"I know what I'm asking," Robin said. "I'm asking you to spare my father's life."

"I do not understand you!" Steel cried, anguish in his voice.

"I know you don't, my friend," Robin said. "But

spare my father's life anyway. Not for his sake, but for mine."

For several agonizing seconds, no one moved. Then, with a great roar of fury and despair, Steel shifted his aim and let the arrow fly. It flashed in the late afternoon sun, streaking over Duke Guy's head, and was lost to sight.

"You have killed us all," Steel said, and I could not tell if he was speaking to me or to Robin. Slowly he sank to his knees, all the fight gone out of him. "It is over."

"Not quite, I hope," said Robin. He turned back to where Duke Guy towered above us. "It would seem that I have just saved your life, Father. According to custom, you are now in my debt."

"What do you want?" Duke Guy asked harshly.

"I want you to give this young woman what she has asked for," Robin said. "Let her be paid the bounty. Bring forward the harp."

Duke Guy began to laugh then. In all my life, I'd never heard such a sound. I did not know there could be a laugh with neither humor nor joy.

"You are a fool, my son. You could have asked for your freedom and I would have been bound to bestow it."

Robin said nothing.

"Oh, very well," said his father. "Bring out the harp, and let everyone here be witness that my debt is discharged."

At this, the richly dressed man who had been

seated beside the duke unwrapped the bundle in his arms. I caught my breath.

Beautiful, so beautiful, I thought.

The lyre gleamed in the late afternoon light, as if made of spun gold. The courtier snapped his fingers, and one of the soldiers brought a chair and placed it beside the duke. The courtier set the harp on the chair, then stepped back, bowing to the duke as he did so.

"Now, young lady," Duke Guy said. "By custom, you must speak your name and the name of the one to whom you will pose your questions. He or she will then be brought."

Now we come to it, I thought. I did not dare to look at Robin, standing at my side. If I did, I feared I might lose my courage when I had the most need for it. Instead I pulled off the kerchief I'd worn to cover my golden hair and curtsied as my mother had once taught me.

"My name is Gentian des Jardins," I said. "And I would like to question you, my lord."

TWENTY-TWO

Duke Guy started. "Celine," he said in a tortured voice. "Celine Marchand."

"Celine des Jardins," I corrected. "Duke Roland's wife and my mother."

"No," Duke Guy said at once. "I do not believe you. It is impossible."

"Believe what you like, as long as you answer my questions," I said.

"No!" Robin's father suddenly shouted. "This is trickery, and I will have none of it. I am Guy de Trabant, lord of this realm. I will not be questioned like some commoner."

"So it's as I've always suspected," Robin said. "Your word means nothing."

"How dare you say so?" demanded his father. "Do you defend the very woman who betrayed you?"

"No," Robin replied. "I defend our family's honor.

To the one who names me, three questions before the harp. *Three questions asked of anyone in the realm.* Was this not your own decree?"

"Yes," Duke Guy said heavily. "You know it was."

"Then honor your word," Robin said simply. "How difficult can it be to answer three questions, Father? When they are over, you'll still have plenty of time to decide what to do with all of us."

"Ask your questions, then," Duke Guy snapped. "But I warn you, do not try to be too cunning. It is not simply in the answers that the harp can detect a falsehood."

"Here is my first question," I said. "Duke Guy de Trabant, have you achieved your heart's desire?"

Duke Guy opened his mouth, then closed it again. I thought I saw his throat work as he swallowed. *Is he swallowing down the lie he wishes to tell?* I wondered.

"No." He bit off the single syllable.

At this, the harp sent up a melody, as pure and ringing as a church bell. And then, to my astonishment, even though I thought I knew what to expect, the harp sounded again.

"He speaks the truth," it sang out.

I heard a sound like the rush of the sea and realized it was the sigh of the crowd.

"Duke Guy de Trabant," I continued, "do you love your son?"

From his position still kneeling at Robin's side, I saw Steel's head turn toward me.

"Ah," Steel said on a sigh. His voice was so low that

only Robin and I could hear it. "I see where you are going, Gen. How I have misjudged you!"

"I know my own name," Robin's father barked in an irritated voice. "You don't have to keep spouting it at me."

"Answer the question," I insisted. *"Do you love your son?"*

"It's ridiculous," Duke Guy sputtered. "You throw a good question away. Ask a different one."

"And I say I will not," I said. "I like this question just fine. But I am beginning to think you do not wish to answer it. Is it because you know you cannot lie?"

"Of course I love him," Guy de Trabant snapped. "Why else would I place a bounty on his head?"

"He speaks the truth," the harp sang out once more.

The final leap of faith was before me now. Either it would carry Robin, Jack, and me to safety, or we would lose it all.

"If I can propose a way to give you back your son, a way to restore your honor in his eyes, will you take whatever bargain I offer?"

This time the answer came without hesitation.

"Yes," said Robin's father.

"Truth. He speaks the truth," the harp sent up its call.

"You have had your three questions," Guy de Trabant said. "Now answer one of mine: What can you possibly have to offer that I will want to accept?"

"Peace," I replied. "Peace for your heart and prosperity for your realm. Let your kingdom truly be united with that of Duke Roland's. You took his lands by bloodshed, by betrayal, and by stealth. You won it all, but still you did not win your heart's desire. But it is not too late. You can still make amends."

"How?" Guy de Trabant asked, and in his voice I heard the torment of hope. *"How can this be done?"*

"Marry your son to Duke Roland's heir. Unite the two kingdoms not through deceit and bloodshed, but through love and honor. Join the two families together; earn the respect of your people; win back the love of your son."

"Your words are fine, but they are nonsense!" Duke Guy exclaimed. He shot a glance in Jack's direction. "I can hardly marry Duke Roland's heir to my son."

"As a matter of fact, you can," Jack spoke up. "Gen is the true heir. She's five minutes older than I am."

A curious expression swept over the duke's face. Despair and hope seemed to fight for possession of it. Then I saw his shoulders sag.

We have won, I thought.

"And you, my son," Guy de Trabant asked. "What say you to this plan?"

I held my breath. I had not told Robin what I intended to propose. I had said only that I would claim the bounty and use the three questions to secure our release.

"I will accept it," Robin said without hesitation. But I could not read his voice. Did he accept the terms because there was no other choice? Or because in his heart it was what he wanted for himself?

"Then let it be so," Duke Guy said. He raised his

arms. "Hear me now, all of you," he cried. "I hereby renounce my crown in favor of my son and Duke Roland's daughter. May their union bring what I desired but could not achieve: prosperity, harmony, and joy."

The crowd began to cheer with a huge upswell of elation. Duke Guy lowered his arms.

"I assume you will make some provision for me," he said with a tired smile. "Come to the castle, all of you, and we will determine what must be done." He turned to the soldiers, who stood, somewhat uncertainly now, around Jack. "Release Duke Roland's son."

The moment Jack's bonds were cut, he leaped from the platform to catch me in his arms.

"So, Gen," he whispered, as he held me close. "It looks to me as if you've had an adventure after all."

"I've had all the adventure that I care to," I said as I hugged him in return. "And it's still all your fault."

TWENTY-THREE

In the end, it was simple. Duke Guy accepted one of the remaining magic beans and agreed to go into exile in the World Below.

The day following the archery contest, Robin and his father set out early, to a place of Duke Guy's choosing. I did not know where it was. But there, the man who had been responsible for my mother's retreat from the World Above threw a magic bean over his left shoulder. Father and son remained together throughout the morning. The top of the beanstalk appeared in the World Above just as the sun was at its highest point in the sky.

The two waited until the beanstalk was tall enough and sturdy enough to take Duke Guy's weight. Then, like my mother before him, Robin's father swung himself onto the beanstalk and disappeared from view, on his way to an uncertain future in the World Below.

"It's almost as if he was relieved," Robin said, late that afternoon. We were walking through the Greenwood once more, on our way to the Boundary Oak. Making this pilgrimage had been my idea, but Robin had agreed to the expedition at once.

Robin and I had not seen much of each other since our victory. He had spent much of his time with his father in private, or conferring with Steel and his father's councillors. Robin was Robin no longer. He was Duke Robert de Trabant now.

"My refusal to live life on his terms changed my father, I think," Robin continued slowly, as if he was still sorting the whole thing out. "When you posed your questions, he could not deny that you were right: He had not achieved his heart's desire. He'd done just the opposite. He'd killed the man he loved like a father; he'd alienated his only son. And then, when I saved his life . . ."

Robin shook his head, as if he still couldn't quite believe all that had transpired.

"How did you know? How did you know what to ask? How did you know my father better than I did myself?"

"I knew you, or at least I hoped I did," I answered simply, though I felt my legs quiver, as if I were stepping out onto uneven ground. "I saw that you loved your father. I simply gambled that the opposite was true, that he loved you as well. That the bounty on your head was more than just a punishment. It was a way to bring you back to him."

I would do almost anything to bring you back, if I believed that I had lost you, I thought.

"Well," Robin said. "It's clear that you were right, for here we are. Though I must say, I'm not quite sure I feel ready to rule a kingdom."

"Surely not all of your father's ministers are corrupt," I said.

"Some, but not all," Robin agreed.

"And you still have Steel. I'm so sorry to have caused him pain. Sorry there was no way to explain what I intended to do ahead of time. But I didn't conceive the plan until you and I were at the Boundary Oak, and by then, Steel had already departed. How long do you think it will take before he fully forgives me?"

"Not as long as it takes him to forgive himself for having doubted you."

"I owe you an apology as well," I continued, my words coming out in a rush. "I'm sorry I didn't tell you the full extent of my plan ahead of time. I knew what I hoped, but even I couldn't be entirely sure of how things would turn out. If your father had answered the first two questions any other way . . ."

"Are you trying to say you do not wish to marry me?" Robin asked quietly.

"No, of course not. I'm trying to say *you* don't have to if *you* don't want to," I stumbled on. "You could just be duke all on your own. The people will follow you. They love you, Robin."

"But you don't. Is that what you're trying to say?"

"Stop putting words in my mouth! I haven't said that at all."

"So you do love me, then," Robin said.

"Don't be silly, of course I do," I said. "I just—"

Robin turned then and pulled me into his arms. "Gen des Jardins," he said, "be quiet. Do you want to marry me or not?"

"Robert de Trabant, make up your mind. I can't be quiet and answer your question all at the same time."

"Yes, you can," Robin said. And then he put his lips on mine.

Jack had said I'd had quite an adventure, and he'd been right. But I can tell you that the first kiss that Robin and I shared was the biggest adventure of all. For it was a promise of the future that lay before us, all the adventures that were still to come.

"That'll teach you to call me silly," Robin murmured against my hair when the kiss was over. "And for the record, I'm not. You are. Of course I want to marry you, you impossible girl from the World Below. I want to marry you because I love you with all my heart. I think I may have loved you from the moment you fell off that sorry excuse for a horse."

"So that's it, then," I said. "This is happily ever after?"

"This is it," Robin answered. "Today and all our days to come. Now, if you don't mind, I'd like to see the Boundary Oak."

Hand in hand, we approached the rise.

"Look!" I cried. "Oh, look, Robin!"

The Boundary Oak was no more. Overnight the great tree had split in two. The two halves had toppled and lay in opposite directions on the ground. But from the center a sapling had sprouted. Its green leaves shimmered in the late-afternoon light. Autumn was not usually a time of year for new things to grow. Still, there was something magical about this little tree.

"Even the oak knows it is a new beginning," I said softly.

"Yes," Robin agreed. "And the tree no longer marks a boundary, for now our two lands are truly one. Wherever he is, I hope my father makes as good a new beginning as this."

"And so do I."

We camped beside the young tree that night, one last night spent under the stars. Then, in the morning, we returned to the de Trabant castle and our own new beginning. The happily ever after of one day, and then the next, through all the days of our lives.

Epilogue

A good plan is like a well-wrapped present. Self-contained, even if it doesn't always get tied with a pretty bow. Still, part of being self-contained is having no loose ends. And even though Robin and I ended up together, which was a lovely conclusion to my adventure, I have to admit that the story as I've just told it does leave a few things out.

Take my mother, for instance. Of course she did not remain in the World Below. As soon as Robin and I had settled things between us, and Jack and Shannon had done the same, Jack tossed his magic bean over his shoulder and returned to the World Below.

Eager to see the place for herself, Shannon clambered down right after him, a choice that made me love her all the more. One week later, first the top of Jack's head, then the top of Shannon's, and finally the top of my mother's head appeared. After sixteen years, Celine Marchand was finally home. She rode to Robin's castle perched on Verité's broad, swayed back, looking every inch the duchess that she was.

Though Robin and I were both on hand to greet her, it was Steel who helped my mother to dismount, going down on one knee before her as soon as both of her feet were firmly on the ground.

"My lady," he said. "I don't expect you to remember me, but . . ."

"But I do know you," my mother answered, wonder in her tone. "You are the seneschal's son . . . Gerard. My husband loved you well."

Steel looked up into my mother's face, the tears plain in his eyes. "As I loved him," he replied. "It would be my very great honor to serve you, my lady, in whatever capacity you care to name."

"Now wait just a minute," Robin protested.

And suddenly all of us were laughing. Steel got to his feet. My mother gave him her hand.

"Let me think on the matter," she said. "I would hate to alienate the new duke by stealing away the friend he needs the most."

My mother did think about it, and apparently doing this required that she spend large amounts of time in Steel's company. A week after the double wedding that united Jack and Shannon, and Robin and me, Mama and Steel departed together for the castle that had once been my mother's home. Her adventure, her new life, doesn't have a happily ever after just quite yet, but even I can see the path that it might take to her door.

And what of Sean? He makes his home in the Greenwood, by the riverbank where Shannon and I slept our first night in the forest, keeping his eye on the top of that last beanstalk. That is where Jack threw his last bean, the one that brought Mama back to the World Above. But with Mama, Jack, and Shannon all climbing up together, there was no one in the World Below to chop down the beanstalk.

Someday, perhaps, another girl seeking adventure will find it. She, too, will climb up a magic beanstalk to discover what lies above.

And if she doesn't, there's still one magic bean left. Robin and I keep it right were Mama did, in a white sugar bowl decorated with pale pink roses. She gave it to us as a wedding present, along with the portrait of her and my father. The painting now hangs in our own great hall. The sugar bowl sits on my dressing table, its contents safe and sound. The magic bean waits, patiently, for the next adventure to come along.

Wild Orchid

CAMERON DOKEY

When the wild wood orchids bloom in the spring, pushing their brave faces from beneath the fallen leaves of winter, that is when mothers like to take their daughters on their knees and sing to them "The Ballad of Mulan," the story of the girl who saved all of China. For if you listen closely to the syllables of that name, this is what you'll hear there: *mu*—"wood"; *lan*—"orchid."

Listening is a good habit to learn for its own sake, as is the art of looking closely. All of us show many faces to the world. No one shows her true face all the time. To do that would be dangerous, for what is seen can also be known. And what is known can be out-maneuvered, outguessed. Lifted up, or hunted down. Uncovering that which is hidden is a fine and delicate skill, as great a weapon for a warrior to possess as a bow or a sword.

I sound very wise and knowledgeable for someone not yet twenty, don't I?

I certainly didn't sound that way at the beginning of my adventure. And there are plenty of times even now when wise and knowledgeable is not the way I sound, or feel. So what do I feel? A reasonable question, which deserves an honest answer.

I feel . . . fortunate.

I have not led an ordinary life, nor a life that would suit everyone. I took great risks, but because I did, I also earned great rewards. I found the way to show my true face freely, without fear. Because of this, I found true love.

Oh, yes. And I did save China.

But I am getting very far ahead of myself.

I was born in the year of the monkey, and I showed the monkey's quick and agile mind from the start, or so Min Xian, my nanny, always told me. I shared the monkey's delight in solving puzzles, its ability to improvise. Generally this took the form of escaping from places where I was supposed to stay put, and getting into places I wasn't supposed to go. My growing up was definitely a series of adventures, followed by bumps, bruises, and many scoldings.

There was the time I climbed the largest plum tree on our grounds, for instance. When the plum trees were in bloom, you could smell their sweetness from a distance so great I never could figure out quite how far it was. One year, the year I turned seven, I set myself a goal: to watch the highest bud on the tallest tree become a blossom. The tallest tree was my favorite. Ancient and gnarled, it stood with its feet in a stream that marked the boundary between my family's property and that of my closet friend—my only friend, in fact—a boy named Li Po.

Seven is considered an important age in China. In our seventh year, childhood comes to an end. Girls begin the lessons that will one day make them proper young women, and boys begin the lessons that will make them proper young men.

Li Po was several months older than me. He had already begun the first of his lessons, learning to read and write. My own would be much less interesting—as far as I was concerned, anyway. I would be taught to weave, to sew, and to embroider. Worst of all was the fact that all these lessons would occur in the very last place I wanted to be: indoors.

So in a gesture of defiance, on the morning of my seventh birthday, I woke up early, determined to climb the ancient plum tree and not come down until the bud I had my eye on blossomed. You can probably guess what happened next. I climbed higher than I should have, into branches that would not hold my weight, and, as a result, I fell. Old Lao, who looked after any part of the Hua family compound that Min Xian did not, claimed it was a wonder I didn't break any bones. I had plummeted from the top of the tree to the bottom, with only the freshly turned earth of the orchard to break my fall. The second wonder was that I hit the ground at all, and did not fall into the stream, which was shallow and full of stones.

Broken bones I may have been spared, but I still hit the earth with enough force to knock even the *thought* of breath right out of my lungs. For many moments all I could do was lie on my back, waiting for my breath to return, and gaze up through the dark branches of the tree at the blue spring sky beyond. And in this way I saw the first bud unfurl. So I suppose you could say that I accomplished what I'd set out to, after all.

Another child might have decided it was better, or at least just as good, to keep her feet firmly on the ground from then on. Had I not accomplished what I'd wanted? Could I not have done so standing beneath the tree and gazing upward, thereby saving myself the pain and trouble of a fall?

I, of course, derived another lesson entirely: I should practice climbing more.

This I did, escaping from my endless lessons whenever I could to climb any vertical surface I could get my unladylike hands on. I learned to climb, and to cling, like a monkey, living up to the first promise of my horoscope, and I never fell again, save once. The exception is a story in and of itself, which I will tell you in its own good time.

But in my determination not to let gravity defeat me I revealed more than just a monkey's heart. For it is not only the animal of the year of our births that helps to shape who we are. There are also the months and the hours of our births to consider. These contribute animals, and attributes, to our personalities as well. It's important to pay attention to these creatures because, if you watch them closely, you will discover that they are the ones who best reveal who we truly are.

I was born in the month of the dog.

From the dog I derive these qualities: I am a seeker of justice, honest and loyal. But I am also persistent, willing to perform a task over and over until I get it right. I am, in other words, *dogged*. Once I've set my heart on something, there's no use trying to convince me to give it up—and certainly not without a fight.

But there is still one animal more. The creature I am in my innermost heart of hearts, the one who claimed me for its own in the hour in which I was born. This is my secret animal, the most important one of all.

If the traits I acquired in the year of my birth are the flesh, and the month of my birth are the sinews of who I am, then the traits that became mine at the hour of my birth are my spine, my backbone. More difficult to see but forming the structure on which all the rest depends.

And in my spine, at the very core of me, I am a tiger. Passionate and daring, impetuous, longing to rebel. Unpredictable and quick-tempered. But also determined and as obstinate as a solid wall of *shidan*—stone.

Min Xian, who even in her old age possessed the best eyesight of anyone I ever knew, claims she saw and understood these things about me from the first moment she saw me, from the first time she heard me cry. Never had she heard a baby shriek so loudly, or so she claimed, particularly not a girl.

It was as if I were announcing that I was going to

be different right from the start. This was only fitting, Min Xian said, for different is precisely what I was. Different from even before I drew that first breath; different from the moment I had been conceived. Different in my very blood, a direct bequest from both my parents. It was this that made my uniqueness so strong.

I had to take Min Xian's word for all of this, for I did not know my parents when I was growing up. My father was the great soldier Hua Wei. Throughout my childhood, and for many years before that, my father fought bravely in China's cause. Though it would be many years before I saw him face-to-face, I heard tales of my father's courage, discipline, and bravery from the moment my ears first were taught to listen.

My mother's name I never heard at all, just as I never saw her face nor heard her voice, for she died the day that I was born.

But the tale of how my parents came to marry I did hear. It was famous, repeated not just in our household but throughout all China. In a time when marriages were carefully arranged for the sake of family honor and social standing, when a bride and groom might meet in the morning and be married that same afternoon, my parents had done the unthinkable.

They had married for love.

It was all the emperor's doing, of course. Without the blessing of the Son of Heaven, my parents' union would never have been possible. My father, Hua Wei, was a soldier, as I have said. He had fought and won many battles for China's cause. In the years before I was born and for many years thereafter, our northern borders were often under attack by a fierce, proud people whom we called the Huns. There were many in our land who also called them barbarians. My father was not among them.

"You must never call your enemy by a name you choose for him, Mulan," he told me when we finally met, when I was all but grown. "Instead you must call him by the name he calls himself. What he chooses will reflect his pride; it will reveal his desires. But what you choose to call him will reveal your fears, which should be kept to yourself, lest your enemy find the way to exploit them."

There was a reason he had been so successful against the Huns, according to my father. Actually, there was more than one: My father never underestimated them, and he recognized that, as foreign as they seemed, they were also men, just as he was a man. Capable of coveting what other men possessed. Willing to fight to claim it for themselves. And what the Huns desired most, or so it seemed, was China.

To this end, one day more than a year before I was born, the Son of Heaven's best-loved son was snatched away by a Hun raiding party. My father rescued him and returned him to the safety of his father's arms. In gratitude the Son of Heaven promoted Hua Wei to general. But he did not stop there. He also granted my father an astonishing reward.

"You have given me back the child who holds the first place in my heart," the emperor told my father. "In return, I will grant the first wish your heart holds."

My father was already on his knees, but at the Son of Heaven's words he bowed even lower, and pressed his forehead to the ground. Not only was this the fitting way to show his thanks, it was also the perfect way for my father to cover his astonishment and give himself time to think. The boy that he had rescued, Prince Jian, was not yet ten years old and was not the emperor's only son. There were two older boys who might, as time went on, grow to become jealous of the fact that their younger brother held the greatest share of the Son of Heaven's heart.

At this prince's birth the soothsayers had proclaimed many omens, none of them understood in their entirety, for that is the way of such prophecies. One thing, however, seemed as clear as glass: It was Prince Jian's destiny to help determine the fate of China.

"My heart has what it desires, Majesty," my father finally said. "For it wants nothing more than to serve you."

It was a safe and diplomatic answer, at which it is said that the Son of Heaven smiled.

"You are doing that already," he replied. "And I hope you will continue to do so for many years to come. But listen to me closely: I command you now to choose one thing more. Do so quickly or you will make me angry. And do not speak with a courtier's tongue. I would have your heart speak—it is strong, and you have shown me that it can be trusted."

"As the Son of Heaven commands, so I shall obey," my father promised.

"Excellent," the emperor said. "Now let me see your face."

And so, though he remained on his knees, my father looked into the Son of Heaven's face when he spoke the first wish of his heart.

"It is long past time for me to marry," Hua Wei said. "If it pleases you, I ask that I be allowed to choose my own bride. Long has my heart known the lady it desires, for we grew up together. I have given the strength of my mind and body to your service gladly, but now let my heart serve itself. Let it choose love."

The Son of Heaven was greatly moved by my father's words, as were all who stood within earshot. The emperor agreed to my father's request at once. He gave him permission to return to his home in the countryside. My parents were married before the week was out. They then spent several happy months together, far away from the bustle of the court and the city, in the house where my father had grown up. But all the time the threat of war hung over their happiness. In the autumn my father was called back to the emperor's service to fight the Huns once more.

My father knew a baby was on the way when he departed. Of course, both my parents hoped that I would be a boy. I cannot fault them for this. Their thinking on the subject was no different from anyone else's. It is a son who carries on the family name, who cares for his parents when they grow old. Girls are gifts to be given in marriage to other families, to provide *them* with sons.

My young mother went into labor while her beloved husband was far away from home. If he had stayed by her side, might she have lived? Might she have proved strong enough to bring me into the world and still survive? There's not much point in asking such questions. I know this, but even so . . . I cannot help but wonder, sometimes, what my life would have been like if my mother had lived. Would I have learned to be more like other girls, or would the parts of me that made me so different still have made their presence felt?

If my mother had lived, might my father have come home sooner? Did he delay his return, not wishing to see the child who had taken away his only love, the first wish of his innermost heart?

When word reached him of my mother's death, it is said my father's strong heart cracked clean in two, and that the sound could be heard for miles around, even over the noise of war. For the one and only time in his life, the great general Hua Wei wept. And from that moment forward he forbade anyone to speak my mother's name aloud. The very syllables of her name were like fresh wounds, further scarring his already maimed and broken heart.

My mother had loved the tiny orchids that grow in the woods near our home. Those flowers are the true definition of "wild"—not just unwilling but *unable* to be tamed. A tidy garden bed, careful tending and watering—these things do not suit them at all. They cannot be transplanted. They must be as they are, or not at all.

With tears streaming down his cheeks my father named me for those wild plants—those *yesheng zhiwu*, wild wood orchids. In so doing he helped to set my feet upon a path unlike that of any other girl in China.

Even in his grief my father named me well, for the name he gave me was *Mulan*.

About the Author

CAMERON DOKEY is the author of more than thirty young adult novels. Her most recent titles in the Once upon a Time series include *Winter's Child*, *Wild Orchid*, *Belle*, and *Before Midnight*. Her other Simon & Schuster endeavors include a book in the Simon Pulse Romantic Comedies line, *How NOT to Spend Your Senior Year*. Cameron lives in Seattle, Washington.

LOOKING FOR THE PERFECT BEACH READ?

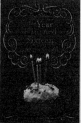

Love. Heartbreak.
Friendship. Trust.

after the kiss
Terra Elan McVoy
author of Pure

From Simon Pulse
Published by Simon & Schuster

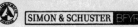